Strebor Quickiez

AUCTIONED

AN INVITATION EROTIC ODYSSEY

A NOVEL

KIMBERLY KAYE TERRY

SBI

STREBOR BOOKS

NEW YORK LONDON TORONTO SYDNEY

SBI

Strebor Books
P.O. Box 6505
Largo, MD 20792

This book is a work of fiction. Names, characters, places and incidents are products of the author's imagination or are used fictitiously. Any resemblance to actual events or locales or persons, living or dead, is entirely coincidental.

ISBN-13: 978-1-61523-152-2

First Strebor Books trade paperback edition March 2009

Cover design: www.mariondesigns.com
Cover photograph: © Keith Saunders/Marion Designs

Manufactured in the United States of America

Dedication

This is dedicated to my beautiful daughters. The first two, in heaven, inspired me to begin this journey of writing. The third, whom I'm blessed to have here on earth, continually motivates me to be the best that I can be.

Nyame-nti
Imandhan

Nyame-nti is an adinkra symbol of south Africa.
It means by God's grace.

ACKNOWLEDGMENTS

I'd like to first thank Madam Zane for diggin' the concept of an Invitation Erotic Odyssey.

I'd also like to thank Charmaine for all of her hard work and attention to details, that helped to make *Auctioned* the best that it could be!

And last, but not least, to two women whom I love and admire, Delilah Devlin and Allison Hobbs—it was a pleasure to work with you two crazy, talented, erotica divas!

Much love,

Kimberly

CHAPTER 1

"Look, I want that report on my desk now. Not in the next couple of hours, not tomorrow, or the next day. Now." Chase ended the connection in the middle of the new advertising assistant's blabbering and apologizing, not interested in anything the inept man had to say.

Her short, manicured nails flew over her keyboard as she drafted the first marketing plan for the lucrative new account she knew was hers. All of her careful courting would pay off, and the position of president of marketing would be hers once she landed the multimillion-dollar deal.

One corner of her full, mauve-tinted lips hitched up in a smile. Euphoria enveloped her at the thought of occupying the large corner office with the breathtaking view of the downtown Dallas skyline that would come with the promotion.

A near orgasmic shudder of delight coursed through her body.

Her eyes were half-closed behind the small square-framed, designer glasses perched on the bridge of her nose, and a sigh of pleasure escaped from between her pursed lips.

She removed one hand from the keyboard and lightly stroked a hand over the head of the man between her thighs as his head bobbed up and down and his gifted tongue softly lapped the inner lips of her vagina. Although her attention was fully on the screen of her computer, she continued to pet him, encouraging him silently to continue.

She released a very low moan when he captured her plump, blood-engorged clit and suckled it deep into his mouth. When he inserted a finger inside her moist core and pumped in and out, she closed her eyes, bit her fuller bottom lip, but didn't utter a word.

She'd become quite proficient at maintaining silence when needed since her discovery of Javier and his spectacular tongue.

Under her desk, where no one could see—if anyone were to enter her office unannounced, he licked and prodded her, stroked and suckled her cunt with hot delicious strokes, while his fingers delved deep into her core and withdrew her moisture.

He used her juices to rim the puckered hole of her anus, lightly stroking, but not daring to imbed his slender finger all the way inside, plying her pussy and ass until her body began to quake. Her limbs tensed, and the muscles in her vagina clamped in a painful constriction with her orgasm hovering, ready to break free.

But he was careful not to bring her to completion.

He knew better than to do that.

He'd learned over the course of the last months of their association that her release was not his to give.

She no longer had to forcibly move his greedy mouth as he devoured her creaming pussy, desperate to take her to the ultimate little death and to prove something she didn't require from him when she felt the beginnings of her orgasm unfurl.

He'd learned to read the signs her body made when she was dangerously close to orgasm.

She felt the tingling sensation begin to strum through her body, heralding that her release was near.

The walls of her pussy contracted and pulsed in a steady relentless beat, and her limbs began the fine trembling that signaled her body was ready to submit to orgasm.

She moaned, placing her hands in the thick, silky strands of his hair and ground against his face. As he licked her and suckled her clit so hard, her back arched sharply away from her chair with every slick press of his tongue.

"Enough!" She barked the words softly, yet his marauding tongue refused to obey. With an expertise that made her bite the inside of her cheek to prevent a scream from releasing, he hollowed out his tongue and shoved it deep into her creaming core.

Chase's eyes flew open as realization dawned on how close she was, how close *he* had been, to making her come.

"Enough, goddamn it." She forcibly stopped her orgasm. Her jaw clenched and tightened as she fought for control. Her fingers dug into his scalp, and she grasped handfuls of his hair, pulling his head from between her thighs.

She stared down at him angrily as he sat crouched between her thighs with the evidence of his oral activities smeared over his face.

His breathing was uneven, and his eyes glittered almost maniacally with a look she'd never seen before. It vanished as quickly as it appeared, too quick for her to catalogue and process its meaning.

"Bring the bag," she bit out the words, licking dry lips. Her breathing was labored and harsh, mimicking his as she fought to bring her body back under control.

She pushed away from her desk, and her chair nearly toppled

with the force. But she ignored it as she strode around the desk. Her eyes quickly moved to the closed door, making sure the lock was in place before she turned back to Javier.

With her eyes narrowed, she waited for him to bring the small, pink bag to her and withdraw the contents.

"I'm sorry," he said, his voice low and husky. His eyes averted from hers in submission as he handed her the dainty beribboned bag.

"Look at me, Javier," she said in a tight, controlled voice.

When he turned around, she placed a long, slender finger beneath his chin, forcing him to look at her as she ran assessing eyes over his flushed, darkly handsome face, searching for a hint of what she thought she'd seen when she pushed him away.

"Look at me," she demanded again, gentling her voice.

For long moments, their gazes locked, his with a slight fear. She knew her gaze was unflinching and cold.

Slowly she moved her finger down his neck, circled the base of his throat with her long fingers, and applied a slight pressure, until he began to cough.

She smiled, knowing he enjoyed the power play as much as she. Once she asserted her dominance, Chase slowly released her hold.

She feathered her fingers down, past his hard, chiseled chest and stopped at the waistband of his slacks. She kept her eyes glued to his as she unfastened his pants, peeling the edges along the zipper aside and yanked them, along with his briefs, down the length of his legs.

After she removed the bag from his tightly clenched hands, she murmured, "Turn around."

His eyes were bright and shining, an anticipatory gleam in

their dark depths as he licked his lips and did as she requested.

He placed both hands on the edge of the large, mahogany desk and lowered his head, braced himself, and waited.

Lifting her skirt, Chase deftly eased her panties down and attached the long, thick dildo to the harness she wore, nestling the base against her clit, snugly, and grasped him by his lean hips.

Separating the hard, muscled cheeks of his ass, she began to feed him her dick. A low growl of satisfaction came from her lips, accompanied by his moaning cries of welcome.

"Hold on, tight. This won't be easy," Chase promised darkly, her breath fanning the fine hairs at the nape of his neck.

She felt a fine tremor run over his body at her hot words of intent.

Without waiting for a response, her fingers tightened on his hips and drove into him in one deep stroke. Her lips pulled back in a feral grin when he gasped, his body arching sharply against the strength of her invasion.

Once the inner muscles of his walls relaxed, allowing her to press into him as far as she could, Chase allowed him no time to become accustomed to her length. Instead she began to move.

Flexing, surging, and plunging, she rolled her hips, plunging deep into his ass. The feel of the artificial dick spanking against her clit stimulated her and aroused her. As she glanced down at their joined bodies, the sight of her dick easing in and out of him as her hips moved against him aroused her even more.

With her legs braced far apart, she removed one hand from his hip and trailed it around to the front of his body, shoving the ends of his shirt aside to grasp his hard, thick rod in her hand.

She feathered her fingers over the turgid length of his shaft and back to his balls, lightly grasping the twin plum-like spheres in her hands. He moaned when she applied a slight pressure, rolling and massaging them in the palm of her hand before her hand dropped away.

She again grasped his cock in hand, circling the base with her thumb and middle finger, and lightly stroked up the length before using the pad of her thumb to swipe across the tiny eye in the center of the bulbous knob, wiping away his sticky pre-cum.

"Taste it," she encouraged.

After placing her thumb in his mouth, he did as she requested, suckling her thumb and making moaning sounds of delight as he licked her finger clean.

She laughed and removed her thumb from his greedy mouth and grasped his lean hips with both hands, fucking him in long strokes to his accompanying mewling cries of pleasure and pain, so interwoven they blended as one melodious cry of rapture.

Chase delivered a sharp, warning slap on the cheeks of his ass.

Immediately his guttural moans were quieted, becoming small whimpering sighs of pleasure even as he pushed back against her invasion.

Her hips moved with precision, surging in and out of him smoothly, the fire inside of her building, growing, with each drag and pull inside his clenching heat. Chase fucked him in sure, easy glides. He cried out, slamming his hips back against her mound, begging her to do him harder, *deeper*.

Yet she kept her strokes, slow, methodical.

She marinated in him in deliberate, slick strokes, ignoring his fervent moans as he accepted—welcomed—her thrusts, the muscled cheeks of his ass flexing and tensing as she rocked into him.

Chase felt so strong, so alive...so in control as she plunged in and out of Javier. The feeling of being buried deep inside of him was an addictive feeling, downright exhilarating.

She bit the lower rim of her lips to the point of pain, her breathing becoming harsher with each roll of her hips against him.

Her head snapped back, and the corded veins in her neck pulsed and throbbed as she felt her hovering orgasm threatening to break. Instead of pushing it away, as she had when he laved between her thighs, she reached for it.

When her orgasm was seconds from spilling over, she reached around his body with her hand. Gently, yet firmly, she cupped his balls, rolling the spheres in her hand until he released a harsh, keening moan.

She grasped his shaft, ran her hands down the length of the steely pipe, in quick, deadly succession, and he broke. His body jerked and spasmed as his cum—thick, white and hot—spewed like a geyser over her hand.

Chase grit her teeth, clenched her eyes tightly shut, and desperately held on to her control even as her orgasm slammed into her. Unable to hold back, the dam broke, and her cum overflowed, weakening her for that brief moment, so that she had to hang on to his hips as she delivered the last of her thrusts into his quaking body.

When it was over, she laid her chest over his heaving back, blanketing his body for that one moment at peace.

"Thank you," he whispered.

His body fully collapsed on the desk, and Chase's fingers

loosened their death grip on his hips as she drew her body away from his.

"Why…why do you…?" he panted, unable to finish the question as he lay spent and useless, his upper body sprawled on top of her desk.

She ignored his question. She knew he loved having her fat dick working his ass as much as she loved giving it to him.

"Ms. Davidson." Chase's eyes narrowed as she listened to her assistant's voice come over the small discreet intercom on her desk. "I'm sorry to interrupt your…lunch."

"What is it, Christine?"

"Your presence has been requested in the boardroom as soon as you're able."

"I'll be right there," she replied, smoothly easing out of Javier.

She reached inside the dainty, pink bag to lift out a pre-moistened tissue. Carefully she wiped the length of the dildo and tossed the used wipe in the trash bin under her desk before placing the dildo back inside the bag.

She moved away from the prostrate man, deftly removed the harness from her hips, and placed it in one of the drawers of her desk before skimming her hands down the length of her body and tugging her skirt into place.

Turning to look at her reflection in the small, wall-mounted mirror, she quickly pulled out another desk drawer, withdrew her lipstick, and ran the tinted, bulbous end over her lips before placing it back in the drawer.

She rubbed her lips together, then raised her hands to her hair, smoothing away errant strands that had escaped the tight chignon secured at the nape of her neck.

Once satisfied with her appearance, she lifted her leather

carryall, hooked the strap over her shoulder, and walked toward the door.

With her hand on the knob, she turned back around. Javier had gotten up from his prone position and was fumbling with his slacks.

"Don't ever forget who's in control. If you do that again, I won't go so easy on you the next time," she said, letting him know that she was aware of his transgression. Had she not stopped him, he would have brought her to orgasm.

Even from the distance she was from him, she could see his olive-tinted face blanch and a fine tremor course over his body in response to her threat.

With a smile of satisfaction, she turned and left.

CHAPTER 2

"Have a seat, Chastity." William Buford stood when Chastity entered the boardroom. A wide smile creased his fleshy, rosy face as he motioned for Chase to take a seat.

William Buford was one of three senior managers in the marketing firm of Manhattan Buford, and his being in attendance at the meeting definitely alerted Chastity that indeed, she would be joining the ranks of senior managers.

"Thank you, sir," she replied, her confidence soaring. Not only was William Buford in the room, but the other two senior managers were in attendance as well, reconfirming that she was minutes away from being offered the president of marketing position.

After she sat down and accepted the glass of ice water from a waiting attendant, Chastity glanced around the room. She returned the smiles of Lance Buford and Emily Manhattan, both of whom held key positions at Manhattan Buford.

"I'd like to begin by congratulating you on landing the Stratham deal. It was truly a coup for you and the firm. Well done," William Buford continued.

"Thank you, sir. I'm very pleased with the results as well," she replied, feeling proud of not only what she had accomplished but that she'd done so after several others in her department had failed to acquire the account.

"Yes, well, you should be!" Lance chimed in. "In fact, you've been watched carefully, these last few weeks, by not only the partners but also Mr. Baptiste."

Daemon Baptiste was the man who owned controlling shares in Manhattan Buford. Chase, as well as all of the upper management to most of the secretarial pool, knew of him.

Although he'd never been seen in the Dallas, New York, and California offices of Manhattan Buford, he was the driving force behind Manhattan Buford.

He owned controlling stock and held the position of CEO of the firm, yet no one besides the partners knew much about him. Gossip floated around the office—that he was a hardnosed businessman, one of the richest men in the country, and also one of the most reclusive.

Few images of him were seen publicly, and the available ones were profiles or from a distance. Upon learning about him, Chase had been mildly curious and had sought to find out more about him. No personal information could be found. She found only the bare facts, reports in financial documents, and legal transactions.

What she did know was that Baptiste was a billionaire tycoon who acquired failing businesses, invested money and new management, spearheading the turnaround until the business was not only solvent but also immensely profitable. He then turned around and sold it off to the highest bidder in multimillion, even billion-dollar, deals.

Several years ago, when Manhattan Buford had been in jeopardy of going bankrupt, Baptiste bought the company and within a year, had revitalized it, even taking it beyond its previous levels of success.

However, instead of selling, he'd held on for reasons no one knew. He left the daily operations with the original partners; however, his unseen presence was felt.

"Wow, now *I'm* impressed." Chase brought the crystal goblet to her mouth and took a sip of water, hiding the satisfied smile that hovered around her lips.

As the cold liquid eased down her throat, she fought back the giddy feeling of triumph that threatened to make her lose control. But it was all she could do not to jump up from her chair and turn a series of undignified, joyful cartwheels straight down the middle of the expensive, beautiful mahogany table.

Yes, the position was hers. She knew it.

And the fact that Baptiste knew of her was simply icing on the cake.

"However, before we go into all of that, we have to wait for Mr. Serrano," William finished, catching Chase completely off guard and making her smile slip.

"Mr. Serrano? I'm afraid I don't understand." She carefully placed the goblet on the table, turning questioning eyes to the managers.

"Well—"

The door opened at that moment, interrupting whatever William had been planning to say.

Chastity's eyes narrowed slightly, and a sense of foreboding struck her when the assistant brought Javier into the room and quietly exited.

"I'm sorry I was late, gentlemen…Ms. Davidson." First, he gave his shit-eating, groveling smile to the partners before turning his smile to Chase and slyly giving her a wink, one that no one saw but her.

The sense of foreboding increased, and she watched his narrow ass sit down in the offered seat after fastidiously brushing away imaginary wrinkles from the 800-dollar, charcoal-gray Armani suit she'd gifted him last week. For work well done.

Chase continued to watch him as he straightened the cuffs of his shirt. The overhead light hit the shining, fourteen-carat gold-and-diamond encrusted links—the same ones she gave him for Valentine's Day—so that they seemed to wink at her much as he had, mocking her.

"Well, let's get this started, shall we, gentlemen…Chastity?" William Buford glanced around the table and once he was assured all eyes were on him, began to speak.

"Chastity, again, we want to congratulate you on the deal. Amazing job, well done. Absolutely amazing! We've been trying to get the Stratham business for over two years. You step in and seal the deal in less than two months. Brilliant!" He rubbed his large, beefy hands together. A smile of pure greed spread across his fleshy lips, splitting his lips so wide his canine teeth were exposed, giving his features an uncomplimentary, wolfish appearance.

"Yes, well, I did work hard for it. In fact—" Her words were cut off when Javier broke in.

"Yes, she did. To see her in action, see how she worked it, how she so cunningly manipulated them, worked on their emotions, found their weakness, exploited them…in a good way of course, was *truly* amazing," he said with a laugh. The board members laughed along with him.

Chastity grit her teeth as her heartbeat slammed against her chest. The son-of-a-bitch was making her seem like some damn piranha as though she were nothing more than a cutthroat shark.

"Well, I wouldn't quite put it like that," she said, cutting in.

"I'm sorry! I didn't mean it in a bad way! Not at all! I've learned so much...being under your tutelage, Ms. Davidson," he replied, turning his attention toward her, the expression on his face guileless as though butter wouldn't melt in his conniving mouth.

She nodded her head shortly and gave him a tight smile, while clamping down on the impeding feeling of disaster looming.

"Yes, it definitely shows how well you've learned under Ms. Davidson's mentorship, Javier," Maurice's booming, jovial voice cut in. The feeling of doom amplified when he called Javier by his first name.

"Which is why, in great part, Javier owes you a great deal of gratitude."

Chase cocked her head to the side, raising a brow in question, although she already knew, deep inside, exactly what William Buford meant.

She *damn* well already knew.

"As you know, Maurice Hines recently left Manhattan Buford, and with his departure, the position of president of marketing opened."

Chastity glanced around the room of smiling executives; a scream of denial lodged tightly in her throat.

She listened with distant awareness as they ran down Javier's qualifications—an MBA from Harvard with an emphasis in management, graduating at the top of his class along with his brief tenure working at Manhattan Buford where he'd been promoted due to long hours and his talent.

The same qualifications that she possessed and more.

"Although he's been with us a short time, we believe that Javier has what it takes to take over the position; his leadership and education are above reproach. He—"

"That position is mine." Chase broke into William Buford's spiel not wanting to hear another word of his detailed outline of Javier's qualifications.

William stopped, and all eyes turned to Chastity. She saw a mocking glint spark in Javier's dark gaze as he too looked at her.

"Excuse me, Ms. Davidson?"

"With no disrespect intended, sir...That position should be mine."

"Yes, well..." He stopped, and, for a moment, Chase felt a sharp sense of triumph as he floundered, trying to find the right words to say. "Yes, Ms. Davidson, you are very qualified for the position as well. You've proven how—"

"Then why? And why wasn't I told that Javier was in the running for this?" Her question was sharp, to the point, the muscles in her face sore from the tight control she was keeping on herself.

"It wasn't an easy decision, Chastity. But we feel it's the best one," William replied, almost gently. She gazed angrily at him, hating the look of pity she saw in his watery blue eyes.

"Then why?" She could not look at Javier. To do so would make her falter and lose what little control she desperately held on her emotions.

"To be honest, Javier has what we're particularly looking for, for this position."

"Chase, look, you know how much we've wanted to get a foot

in the Latin market. Javier recently has met Roberto Chavez," he said, mentioning the name of a key player in a successful Hispanic-owned and operated advertising agency whose projects included national commercial print and media ads. "With his courting, they are now considering working with us—"

"*Considering*?"

"Yes. Nothing is confirmed. As I said, we feel confident that Javier will be able to bring us the account." A deep red flushed the man's cheeks, and when he couldn't look directly at Chastity, she turned to stare at Javier before turning back to face Buford.

"What the hell is this about? And don't give me that bullshit line that Javier 'has what it takes' to run the position," she said his name with disdain, jerking a thumb in his direction. "That's a line of crap and we all know that. I worked all day, every day, never took one damn day of vacation time, working long nights, then took work home on weekends...making sure the work was done, and done correctly. No matter *who* the hell took off, I was there, working my ass off! I've just landed…not 'considering'…*landed*…a multi-million dollar account and you have the audacity to tell me this shit?"

The room was silent after her outburst. The proverbial pen could have dropped and all would have heard it. No one said a word, the tension in the room so palpable and thick it felt like a noose around her neck.

"We have another position for you, Chastity. One which we feel you will see the merits of, given time—" William Buford was the first to speak.

"And what would that be?"

There was an ominous moment of silence, and Chase watched them exchange nervous-looking glances. There was a wealth of communication in their silent conversation, one that confused her as much as angered her.

"Mr. Baptiste wants you to work with him."

"What?"

"As his assistant."

"*His assistant*?" Chase narrowed her eyes, spearing them with her glance. She carefully took note of the nervous way William played with the tip of his gold-covered fountain pen, and the way Emily Manhattan avoided her eyes. "So, you're telling me, I'm being *demoted?*"

"No! Not at all, please, Ms. Davidson, listen—"

"This is utter and complete bullshit."

"I'm sorry that you feel that way, Chastity. You are a valuable member of this team."

"If I'm so valuable, why am I being demoted to assistant, William? Tell me that!"

"I'm not at liberty to discuss that with you, at this time. Mr. Baptiste himself will be in contact with you—"

"I don't think so. You can tell Mr. Baptiste he can damn well find himself another lackey. I quit."

There was silence in the room, for long minutes. Chastity turned her head away, and fought back the burn of tears she felt threatening to fall, until she heard the scrape of chairs easing against the plush carpeting, indicating the men were leaving the table.

And that was it. No asking her to reconsider, no negotiating, nothing.

One by one, they left the room. Chastity kept her face averted until she heard the sound of the door opening and closing. When she thought they were all gone, she turned back around, and came face to face with Javier.

He smiled and leaned down, whispering in her ear, "Who got screwed now, bitch?"

She clenched her jaw and said nothing. She simply watched him turn around and saunter toward the door before he left the room.

One lone tear escaped, unnoticed, and trailed down Chastity's cheek.

CHAPTER 3

"Hey lady, what's going on? I ain't seen you in a while."

Chase walked into the dark, deserted bar and offered a smile to the man who stood behind the bar wiping down the counter with another towel.

"Not a whole lot, Mickey. What about you?" she asked as she walked inside, stopping when she reached the bar.

She pulled out one of the high bar stools and climbed onto the seat, placing her bag and laptop on the empty stool beside her.

"Can't complain. Wife is out visiting her mama, got the place to myself for a change," he answered, grinning widely and exposing a shining set of pearly-white dentures that glistened starkly against his charcoal-colored skin.

"Yeah, and what are you going to do with all that freedom?" she asked and nodded her head when he put a glass of whiskey in front of her.

"Hmmm. Don't know. Maybe I'll have that orgy I been thinkin' about," he replied and winked.

Chase offered a small smile in return and swirled the shot glass around, the amber-colored liquid swirling around the small chunks of tinkling ice.

"You gonna play with that or actually drink it?" the old man asked in a hoarse voice, thanks to years of smoking and hard drinking.

She lifted the glass to her lips, drank it in one swallow, and shut her eyes as the alcohol burned and slid down her throat.

After she placed the empty glass down, she raised her eyes and caught Mickey staring at her. A thoughtful expression lined his face.

"Fucked-up day at the office?" he asked, nodding his head toward the empty glass, silently asking if she wanted another.

She shook her head "no" to the refill.

"That's putting it mildly." Her laugh rang hollow even to her own ears.

"Wanna talk about it? I've been told I'm a good listener."

Chase sighed and shook her head, still stunned at the turn of events over the last few hours.

"Have you ever had your dreams snatched from you, Mickey? Have you ever been this close?" she asked, putting up two fingers indicating the length span of an inch. "This close to being number one? And just when the prize is within range, after years of building to that moment, it vanishes. Poof. And you're left freefalling, adrift, and no idea how the fuck it happened?" Chase laughed a harsh-sounding laugh, shaking her head. "Well, that's about how I feel right now. All I wanted to be is number one…is that asking too much?" Although she voiced the question to Mickey, she knew he didn't know the answer to the question, and was speaking to herself more than him.

"Sorry. Yeah…it's been one of those kind of days," she finished. "Look, I'd better go." She glanced up at him as she spoke. The forced smile that she had put on began to slide off her face when she noticed the intent way he was looking at her.

"Hey, why don't you stick around a bit more? Like I said, I'm a good listener," he offered, again, a look of worry creasing his wide forehead.

"No." She wrinkled her nose. "I'm sure you are. I think I've opened up more than enough for one day. But thanks for the offer." She smiled.

He opened his mouth to speak, but promptly closed it. "Why don't you let me make you another drink, one of my specialties? Cures the blues…I even heard it can cure the common cold." He laughed hoarsely.

"Does all that, huh?" She raised a brow. "No, but do you have anything good in the back? Something I can take home with me?"

The surprised look on his face almost made her laugh.

She rarely drank besides an occasional social glass and in the two years she'd known Mickey, he'd never seen her drink more than a shot or two at the most.

"Like I said…It's been a real bitch of a day."

He cocked his head to the side, as though considering something.

"I got just the thing for you. I ordered a few boxes of some real fancy shit last week for some rich guy giving a party: 2001 Cabernet Sauvignon—it just came in. He won't know the difference if I take out a bottle or two."

"For a price, right?"

"You know it, Boo." He laughed, winking at her. His rotund, stout body ambled away toward the back and moments later he returned with a bottle of the wine, offering it to her for her inspection.

"Hmmm. Nice," she murmured, taking the bottle from his

hand and cradling it in her hand, the bottle neck nestled in her palm; the base, cool…soothing…against her inner arm.

"What do I owe you?" she asked, jumping from the barstool and grabbing her things from the stool beside her.

"It's on the house."

"Come on, what do I owe you, Mickey?" She raised incredulous eyes toward him.

"Take it and go before I change my mind." He winked, and with a grin, she thanked him and turned to leave.

She was on her way out of the door when Mickey's voice stopped her.

"You know, being number one can come with a high price. Some would say a harsh price. Are you ready to pay that price, Chase?"

She stared at the door, considering his question. "I've been ready for a long time, Mickey," she answered without turning around.

CHAPTER 4

"What good are you? Can't even fucking tie your goddamn shoe! Come here!"

Chastity's small frame was hauled close to her mother by her collar. With angry, precise movements, her mother tied her shoe, pulling the laces so tightly they dug into the top of her foot. When she was finished, Maybelle shoved her away, and Chastity stumbled, nearly falling.

But, she caught herself, fought for balance, knowing that if she were to fall her mother's anger would escalate.

She controlled her balance as well as the tears burning the back of her throat as she looked at her mother's angry face. Despite her dark complexion, the blush of anger was visible on her jet-black skin.

"You ain't no damn good. Just like *him*," the angry woman muttered, her features tight, her eyes filled with an ugly hatred. The nostrils of her large nose flared in her utter disgust of the small girl.

Chastity carefully avoided her mother's direct stare, casting her eyes aside, staring down at the toe of her scuffed, second-hand sneakers. She was confused and unsure of what she'd done to anger her mother this time.

At the age of seven, Chastity had learned to dare not question her mother. She'd learned to take the insults, the scorn, the smacks, the punches, and the hits all in stride.

She'd also learned to hold herself very still, not look directly into her mother's eyes, and refrain from angering her mother more. The added tears or stupid questions asking what she'd done to make Momma mad, the more likely she was not to get a beating.

The more likely her mother was to just insult her until she grew tired and leave Chastity alone in her room.

She felt Momma's malevolent glare, and her body trembled as it always did.

So afraid.

Her mother was a frightening woman, just one look from her, and Chastity wanted to run and hide. Maybelle was so big, so tall, and so scary when she was angry.

Chastity glanced down at herself, hating how small *she* was, much smaller than the other children in her second-grade class. Her teacher, Ms. Mosley, had told her today that she was so cute and tiny, that she looked like she belonged in pre-school.

Chastity had looked at the woman, without a smile on her small face, and told Ms. Mosley that she wasn't a child.

A strange expression had settled across the woman's pretty face as she stared down at the little girl. Her eyes moved over Chastity's face, her exposed, deep brown-colored, skinny arms with a multitude of healing purplish bruises, down her slight body and legs so skinny the white knee socks she wore bagged helplessly around her little ankles, and the woman's eyes misted.

She remembered how sad she'd felt for Ms. Mosley, feeling bad that she'd somehow made her cry.

Chastity had sought to console her, placing a frail arm around the woman's waist.

The hug Ms. Mosley had given her in return had been the first time anyone had hugged her in her life that she could remember.

It felt good. Warm. Strange, yet…good.

"Are you listening to me, girl? You ain't no damn good!"

Chastity felt her mother's warm, pungent, sour breath fan the hair on the side of her neck as Maybelle leaned down to whisper the ugly words against her ear.

Nodding her head up and down in assent, Chastity immediately spoke when her mother cuffed her face with a closed fist, reminding her that she was to verbally acknowledge to her mother that she was pitiful. That she was less than.

"Yes, ma'am," she spoke, her voice barely above a whisper, and stopped, clearing her throat. "Yes, ma'am, I know."

Chase woke with a start, her heart thudding an erratic beat against her chest. She came to full wakefulness out of a series of vivid dreams, a kaleidoscope of times gone by, times where she was hopeless and afraid.

A time she did her damnedest to never consciously re-visit during her lucid moments. Yet a time that she'd never been able to shake in her dreams.

Her head pounded with pain. She glanced over, barely able to make out the empty wine bottle on her dresser.

"I guess drinking a bottle of wine will do that for you," she mumbled.

In the dark room, the light shafting in through the slates of the wide, wooden blinds on her bedroom's single bay window cast the room in shadows. Shadows that came to blazing life on her wall, grouping and forming lifeless bodies that all seemed to be glaring at her, mocking her with their shadowy, wicked grins.

"Damn," she mumbled, her chest rising and falling heavily.

She untangled the black satin sheets twined around her body, shoved them to the side, and inhaled a deep, calming breath.

After her racing heart had resumed a semblance of normalcy, she reached over and flipped on the dainty bedside lamp on her small, Chippendale nightstand. When the soft light filled her dark bedroom, banishing the shadows, she rested her body against the padded leather headboard.

Before she left the office, after giving her resignation, Chase had gone into her office, walked past her assistant, with her face carefully devoid of any emotion, and told her she was no longer with Manhattan Buford. She had then gone inside, closed the door, and methodically gone through every one of her files.

She removed both paper files and backed up on disc those from her computer before wiping it clean from clients she'd worked with, clients she damn well had every intent of taking with her, wherever that may be.

Then she removed the few personal items in the office, placing them all neatly in her Nike gym bag, and left the office without a backward glance at her astonished assistant.

As soon as she got home from Mickey's, she kicked off her heels, removed her jacket, and tossed it and her leather case on the butcher-block table in the center of the spacious kitchen. She'd quickly stripped down and put on an old pair of running shorts, ripped T-shirt, and her favorite pair of running shoes. Then she took off, running.

She'd had no direction in mind, and to that end, she had simply taken off at a fast clip, running through her small neighborhood. Past the familiar running path she normally took, Chase ran deep into the dense, bushy non-developed area. As she ran, limbs slapped against her legs, the sharp sting going unnoticed as her feet pounded against the dirt and grass, and her long legs carried her across the pavement.

She ran fast and hard, ran until she couldn't run anymore. With her body aching, with every muscle in her body screaming in pain, quivering and shaking, she turned around and slowly jogged the long way back home.

It was late when she got back. Without lights she navigated through her condo and up to her bedroom. The blinking light on the small phone indicated that she had a message. After she stripped out of her clothes, she hit the replay button.

"Did you get it?"

Maybelle did not ask anything else. No greeting, nothing… just those four words.

Yet, those four words, accompanied by the one who asked, made her gut clench, and her hands formed tight fists, her short nails digging small crescent moons into the palms of her hand.

She took the opened bottle of wine Mickey had given her, stripped out of her sweat-drenched clothes and padded naked to the bathroom that joined her bedroom. She lifted the bottle of wine and placed the rim to her lips and drank from it deeply, the spicy, poignant liquid soothing and relaxing her even as it slid down her throat. She finished the bottle, and wearily she had fallen asleep within minutes. And now, here she was awake, restless. And jobless.

"What am I going to do now?" she murmured, turning her head to the small alarm clock with its bright red numbers flashing, and blew out a breath.

Three thirty-five a.m.

Leaning over to the side table, she lifted her glasses, placed them on her nose, and removed her razor-thin laptop from the small stand. Sitting back, she unlatched it and powered up.

"May as well start seeing what's out there, headache or no headache," she said, continuing her one-sided conversation. As secure as she'd been at Manhattan Buford, she always kept her ears opened for what was going on in other firms.

"Not that I thought for one goddamn minute, I'd be in the position I'm in now," she, replied—disgust, anger and a keen sense of betrayal jockeying for position of prominence in her emotions.

Images of her and Javier locked together, his moans and cries of pleasure as she fucked him still ringing in her ears, warred with images of him sitting in the boardroom, a self-satisfied smirk on his handsome face as they named him president of marketing, as he stole her position...her dreams...all of it flashed through her mind's eye.

"The sneaky little son-of-a-bitch." As she bit the words out, she felt her body tense, the muscles in her arms and hands bunch and knot.

She looked down at her hands, balled into fists, and forced her fingers to relax, her hand to open and release the death grip she had on the edges of her laptop.

She shook her head in an attempt to rid her mind of the images, banishing them to the shadow realm, the same place she forced her dreams to go.

She turned her attention to the screen in front of her when she realized her email had turned on when she powered up, a small ding letting her know she had mail. She was seconds from closing down her email server so she could work, when a small envelope appeared with the words *The Invitation* in the subject line.

Something about the simple one-word subject strangely appealed to her.

Despite the thought that it was some bullshit spam email asking her if she was satisfied with the size of her dick, she clicked on the small icon before it could disappear.

The body of the email held a cream-colored envelope, so real looking, so soft in appearance, it appeared as though if she touched the screen, she'd be able to feel the smooth, crisp linen caress her fingers.

Her eyes widened slightly when the envelope became animated, unfurling to reveal a note inside.

The script was one she hadn't seen before, bold, yet feminine in appearance at the same time. Narrowing her eyes she read the contents.

The Invitation…

You are cordially invited to The Island, a place where your strongest desires come to blazing life with just one wish. At The Island, we cater to your most self-indulgent fantasy…where you are number one.

This invitation is given only to a select few, and you've been chosen. Should you choose to accept this invitation, you agree that you are succumbing to your desires, that you are freeing yourself to experience something you've never dared to succumb to. And in doing so, your desire to be number one will manifest deliciously so…

"And the day came when the risk to remain tight in a bud was more painful than the risk it took to blossom."

This invitation will expire in twenty-four hours, Chastity. You can contact us at 800-555-9860 to experience the fantasy of a lifetime.

We're waiting for your call.

"What kind of scam is this?" Chastity murmured, yet felt shaken after she re-read a line in the invitation.

A place where your strongest desires come to blazing life with just one wish...

Her heart began to race, a dizzy feeling swamping over her as she scanned the invitation once more.

Unknowingly she said aloud the phone number in the corner of the invitation, "8005559860." Surprised, she saw it reanimate, refolding in on itself. It became in appearance the unopened envelope, the ends sealing, and again showing only the red embossed seal with an impression of a flower stamped within.

"Wait..." she cried out, frantically, reaching a hand out as though to physically force the envelope to reopen.

Immediately, she felt heat invade her naked thighs where her computer set on her lap. Hissing, she shoved it off her legs and onto the bed beside her.

"Damn!" she grunted, when the laptop toppled off the bed and onto the floor.

Scrambling off the bed she quickly retrieved it, in time to see the animated card twirl, spinning as though it were a kid's spin toy before it disappeared with a zip.

"No!" she cried out, "800-555-9860, 800-555-9860, 800-555-9860." She chanted the number over and over as she yanked the drawer open on her nightstand and frantically searched for something to write the number down on.

She breathed a sigh of relief when she found a pen and pad, and quickly scribbled the number down.

With her heart racing, her lips partially opened as she blew out a gush of air, she sat back and stared at the number.

She turned her head, looking at her cell phone on the nightstand before glancing out of the bedroom window.

It wasn't even dawn.

No way in hell would someone be there to take her call from the travel agency.

Yet, she knew deep down, this was no ordinary travel agency. And she'd bet her considerable severance pay, it wasn't a typical getaway.

She reached for her cell and punched in the number.

A deep voice with no discernible accent answered, "How may I help you, Ms. Davidson?"

Her stomach clenched.

No, this was definitely something out of the ordinary.

Just what I needed, Chase thought.

CHAPTER 5

Chase flew into the Honolulu airport, and a uniformed man with a sign with her name on it greeted her. He escorted her, one hand solicitously under her elbow, to the waiting charter plane that would take her to her final destination.

Now seated, she glanced at the small group of travelers.

Besides her, there were two other women, the pilot, and one attendant. She had expected there would be more.

Chase thought back over her conversation with the man. After she'd gotten over the shock of her impulsiveness by calling the agency, she had been surprised at how the smooth-voiced man had processed her information as though her early morning call was nothing out of the ordinary.

Although he answered all of her questions, a detailed accounting of her travel plans along with a promise to e-mail the information immediately to her, it hadn't been until Chase had gotten off the phone that she'd realized many of his answers had been vague when she asked about specifics regarding certain aspects of the trip.

He informed her that the resort was exclusive, one that wasn't publicly advertised, yet very high end. When she asked how he'd gotten her name, her information, why her…he smoothly told her that a friend had been her benefactor.

"Benefactor?" she questioned.

If the resort was as high end as he said, Chase wondered which "friend" of hers would do something like that for her. She *had* no friends. Definitely not one who had the means or inclination to be her benefactor. "'Benefactor' in that you must be recommended before you can attend the resort, Ms. Davidson. You are responsible for the fee…and everything included, should you choose to accept the invitation."

He told her the fee, and she blanched at the price. For that amount, she could buy a small resort of her own.

"As I said, if you choose to accept the invitation—"

"I do," she cut in, impulsively making the decision.

She heard the smile in his voice as he continued, finishing the transaction and notifying her that she needed to be ready to go in the next twenty-four hours. She would receive everything she needed in the next thirty minutes, instructions as well as her flight itinerary, at that time.

Once she was off the phone, it hit her that not only had she agreed to everything, she hadn't bothered to ask how he knew she would be available to leave that soon. The entire conversation left her in a bemused state.

"Had to be Mickey," Chastity murmured aloud.

As soon as I return, I'm making a beeline for the bar. I have a few questions for Mickey, Chase thought, settling deeper into the comfortable, leather plane seat.

As the plane headed toward the small, private island of Ka-le'a, she glanced out of the window, staring down at the bright blue water and the cluster of islands. It was a breathtaking view.

Ka-le'a was owned and operated by someone by the name of Merrick. It was the only information she'd been able to find out about the island. Chase had no idea if it was owned by some large corporation, or one owner, or if the owner was male or female. The agent hadn't given her any more information about ownership besides giving her the name Merrick.

What he did tell her was that the island was bought several years ago from the Hawaiian government after years of being vacant. The owner or owners had then transformed the deserted island into a closed resort, exclusively available only to those invited.

For Chase, the fact that it was so exclusive that one had to be invited added a certain appeal.

She turned and glanced at the other two women on the plane, running assessing eyes over the one seated in front of her.

The woman was a prima donna of the first order, from the crown of her shining, straight, dark blonde hair, to the tip of her powder-pink polished toes which peeked out from the metallic-silver, strappy Jimmy Choo sandals.

She was a strangely beautiful, exotic contrast. Her skin, the color of brushed copper, looked just as silky and as soft. Her features were boldly African: large, prominent nose; full, sensual lips; and high cheekbones. Her eyes, an unusual shade of green, were startling in their intensity.

She was the last to enter the plane, arriving at least an hour after the scheduled takeoff, escorted by two large muscle-laden men who strangely complemented her unique appearance: one very Nordic-looking man with long thick blond hair that fell to the middle of his broad shoulders; and the other, equally opposing looking, a fiercely handsome African-American man.

When the woman had been told the men couldn't join her on the plane, she'd angrily fought it, demanding to speak to the pilot. After several exhausting, drama-filled minutes, she relented and, with tears streaming down her face, hugged both men tightly in farewell.

Chase had watched the display with open astonishment.

And with a certain amount of unconscious jealousy as she observed how the two men had seemed to treat the tall woman as though she were a fragile, porcelain doll, escorting her onto the plane, demanding to do so, and reluctantly leaving the weeping woman behind.

"Must be rough," Chase mumbled.

"Excuse me?"

"Nothing." She shook her head when the woman sitting closest to her turned large blue, inquisitive eyes her way.

"Oh, sorry," the woman mumbled, taking a final bite of the éclair she'd been eating. She delicately dusted her powdery fingers on a napkin, her glance falling away from Chase.

Chase watched as "Blue Eyes" fiddled with the handle of her purse, placing it in her lap as she opened it and peered inside. Over and over, she opened and closed the purse, moving the items inside its deep cavernous insides as though searching for something, only to re-close it, and do the same thing again.

And again.

Her strange behavior was beginning to irritate Chase. Chase resisted the urge to reach over and snatch the bag away from her small, pale fingers.

Unlike the obviously rich and exotic beauty in the front seat, this one didn't look as though she could afford to take a trip to the grocery store, much less afford the exclusive resort.

She was pretty in a typical "girl next door" type of way. Long, wavy, blonde hair; overly large blue eyes; a small pink mouth shaped in a bow.

She wore a cheap, two-piece beige suit, complete with pantyhose and bland slip-on pumps, all of which had probably come from a discount retail shop. As Chase's critical gaze ran back up the woman's body, their gazes locked.

The woman bit the bottom rim of her lip as she gaped at Chase.

Purposely, Chase grinned, lowered her lids, and stared at the woman's mouth. She kept her gaze steady on the woman; her desire to fluster the fidgeting woman increased the longer the woman stared at her in open fascination.

Obviously unnerved by the attention, the purse slipped from the woman's grasp and fell to the floor. Chase reached over to retrieve it at the same time that the woman did.

Their heads lightly bumped. Chase boldly licked away the chocolate frosting in the corner of the woman's cupid bow-shaped mouth before she could move away. She held back a laugh when the pale woman's eyes widened comically so. She jumped away, grabbed her purse and held it tightly against her chest.

"You had a bit of icing on your mouth," Chase murmured, her grin widening at the look of fear…and interest…that gleamed in the woman's light-blue gaze.

Bored and more than ready to begin her vacation, Chastity turned away from the woman, and within moments, the tepid blonde was forgotten as her thoughts went to the adventure ahead of her.

Watching the water below, a soothing and comforting feeling enveloped Chase, and a strange sense of euphoria washed over her. She closed her eyes, allowing her mind and body to relax for a moment, the first she'd done in a long time. Within minutes, she was asleep.

"Ms. Davidson, we've landed."

Chase's eyes flew open and she jerked upward, instantly disoriented.

"Wha—what?" she stuttered, staring into the face of the smiling flight attendant.

She straightened her body and fumbled with the clasp of her seatbelt, her face flushing when she realized that she'd fallen asleep.

"The water has that effect on a lot of our travelers—particularly our travelers who have a lot on their minds," the woman replied with a glint of understanding in her eyes.

Chase gave the woman a tight smile in return, neither wanting nor needing her sympathy.

As she gathered her things, she noted that her traveling companions had obviously already de-boarded the plane. Quickly, she grabbed the small carry-on that she'd stashed beneath her seat and stood.

She withdrew her sunglasses from her purse and placed the oversized shades on her face. She strode down the aisle, anticipation and excitement churning in her stomach as she thought of the adventure ahead of her.

As soon as she took the last steps off the plane, she glanced in front of her and saw a long, welcoming line, littered with beautiful women wearing typical Hawaiian apparel of two-piece colorful swimsuits exposing taut, golden skin, wide smiles on their golden-brown faces, and colorful leis in their hands as they waited to welcome her.

At the front of the line, a tall man dressed in all white—slacks, jacket and shirt—was watching her, waiting for her to approach as well. At his side, a woman similarly dressed in all white stood.

He held out a hand as she approached, and she stuck her hand out to shake it. He immediately took her hand and softly kissed her palm, sending electric static through her body. Chase felt her nipples bead against the silk blouse she wore. She quickly withdrew her hand, unnerved by her body's strange reaction.

"Welcome to the Island, Ms. Davidson. We've been eagerly waiting your arrival," he spoke in a low voice, one that she instantly recognized.

"You're the one I spoke with…the one who set up my arrangements," she stated, rather than asked, confident that he and the travel agent were one in the same.

He inclined his head in a slight acknowledgment. His fathomless, dark-brown eyes gave nothing away.

Chase ran her eyes over him. At her height of five feet nine, coupled with the three-inch heels she traditionally wore, she was used to being taller than—or at least as tall as—most men. Not so with this one.

He stood a full head taller than her. If Chase had to guess an age, she'd place him in his mid-to-late fifties, mainly because of the steely gray hair covering his head. Yet, no wrinkles lined his distinguished-looking face, and Chase couldn't detect an ounce of discernible flab on his fit-looking body.

"Welcome to Ka-le'a, Ms. Davidson." The petite woman dressed in white at his side moved as though to place the lei in her hands around Chase's neck.

Chase withdrew, not allowing the woman to do so. The man turned his head toward the woman and shook his head slightly. Without a word, the woman's hands dropped to her sides.

"My name is Merrick. If you need anything throughout your stay, please do not hesitate to ask. If you're ready, please allow one of my assistants to escort you to your lodgings," he said, motioning for one of the few male attendants to come forward.

The mention of his name made Chase turn to him in surprise. This was not only the one she'd called, the one who'd set up her arrangements, but he was also the owner of the island.

"Thank you, Mr. Merrick. And yes, I think I am ready."

A smile stretched across her face as she allowed the handsome waiting attendant to take her bags and gallantly grasp her beneath the elbow and lead her away to a waiting small topless, white Jeep. He stored her bags in the back and opened her door for her before jogging to the driver's side and hopping inside.

Chase sat back with a sigh of contentment, enjoying the late afternoon breeze that gently blew over her and listening with half-hearted attention to the guide's commentary about the island.

It was an idyllic scene, one that could be taken straight out of a movie. The palms on the large trees were lazily fluttering, and the air was thick with nature's perfume of wildly growing hibiscuses that grew alongside the road.

As her thoughts turned inward, her guide continued to drive slowly along the empty roadway, pointing out the flowers and plants indigenous to the island.

I could get used to this, Chase thought. *No worries, no fighting to get to the top, no disappointment over missed opportunities, no wondering what to do next*...She determinedly chased the thoughts away.

No, now was not the time to think about any of that. She planned on enjoying her time here to the fullest and eagerly anticipated what the island had in store for her.

"We're here." The guide interrupted her thoughts.

He came to a smooth halt in front of a quaint, sloped-roof cottage, positioned yards away from the road and nestled between tall palms, a scattering of cylinder-shaped papaya trees, and an abundance of floral bushes and low shrubbery.

Chase stared out at the cottage—eager and apprehensive at the same time. Yet she controlled her excitement, taking deep breaths of air, and remained seated as the guide went around the back of the Jeep and removed her luggage, keeping her gaze on the quaint cottage and lush foliage surrounding it.

After he'd gathered her things and opened the door for her, she allowed him to escort her the short distance to the cottage.

Once he'd unlocked the door, he stepped back and allowed her to enter in front of him into the dark, cool interior.

She walked inside, her eyes taking in the simple yet elegant furnishings in the cottage. The cottage was divided into sections by floor-to-ceiling wood beams. The largest area was the living area, where plush sofas and overstuffed chairs dominated the room, along with ceramic-potted ferns placed on low stands.

"I'll put your bags away," the guide said and disappeared into another sectioned-off area, which Chase assumed was the bedroom.

She walked toward the kitchen, her eyes glancing over the small, efficient room before walking toward a closed patio door.

She opened the doors and walked out into the balcony, smiling when she noted the long stretch of beach visible from where she stood, its pristine whiteness gleaming against the late afternoon sun.

"There is a welcome luau scheduled in the next hour. I can return to pick you up. If you would like to attend, simply dial zero on your phone." Chase turned when the guide spoke directly behind her.

"Thank you—wait," she said when he smiled and turned to go. She opened her purse, searching for money to tip him.

He brought a hand up, stalling her. "No, please…That won't be necessary, Ms. Davidson!" A horrified expression crossed his darkly handsome face, as though she'd committed an act of treason. "I am here to serve *you*. There is no need for recompense."

Chase's hands dropped from her purse, and she carefully placed the bag back on the butcher-block counter. "I'm sorry, I just thought—"

"No, it's no problem. As I said, I'm here to serve you. We all are," he murmured, his dark slumberous eyes raking over her body making her feel naked and exposed. The same feeling she'd gotten, the same prickling heat she'd felt when Merrick had kissed her palm.

"Do you need anything else from me, right now?" he asked in such a way that Chase felt her body respond with a primal inner shout of "yes"…

"No, I think that will be all. Thank you," she replied, instead.

After he left her alone, she exhaled her pent-up breath in one long puff.

She withdrew the long pins holding her hair in the tight chignon, throwing the pins on the table before striding from the room. A long, cool shower was in order.

CHAPTER 6

Her body glistened rosily after the long scrubbing she gave it.

The water from the powerful multi-head shower pounded over Chastity's skin, stimulating her as she luxuriated in the large glassed-in shower. She lathered the sweet-smelling soap over her hair as she scrubbed her body until she felt as though she'd scrubbed every last negative thing away.

Although the water hadn't cooled in the thirty minutes she'd allowed the powerful jetting water to sluice over her skin, she reluctantly turned off the tri-head showerhead, opened the glass door, and reached for the soft, thick, cream-colored robe from a nearby hook and wrapped herself within its warm embrace.

The porcelain floor was cool against her feet as she padded over to the vanity. Chastity peered at herself critically in the gold framed mirror that wrapped around the length of the bathroom.

She noted the minute changes in her appearance. The dark circles underscoring her eyes were fainter; the fine lines of tension that seemed to be a permanent fixture around her small mouth were also softer. She ran one finger beneath the slightly darkened skin underscoring her almond-shaped, light-brown eyes. Surrounding her pupils was a ring of gold around her irises.

Cat eyes.

That's what her mother always told her. She had sly, cat eyes. Just like her father.

Her high cheekbones and a long, oval face, she'd gotten from him.

She stroked her tongue over her small lips and examined herself, feathering her fingers over each of her features, as though she was cataloging them, assessing them, and looking for flaws.

She ran a finger down the short bridge of her nose, over full, naturally blushed lips, and along the slight yet discernible dimple in her chin.

That she'd gotten from her father also.

On the outside, she was the feminine image of her father. She had a tall, athletic body, one she spent hours in the gym to maintain. She lifted one of her heavy breasts, breasts she'd painfully begun developing at an early age, thumbing a finger over the flat disk of her areole, lightly feathering a thumb over her nipple that was becoming stiff and erect with her light touches.

She opened the robe further and stroked her hands down her body, one hand lifting a breast, the other venturing past the tight muscles of her abdomen, the swell of her hips, before traveling to the trimmed thatch of hair between her thighs.

With detached awareness, she watched herself in the mirror as she parted the slick folds and ran one lone finger between the lips, circling her clitoris in tight swirls and back again.

She closed her eyes, and moaned lightly, one hand buried in her pussy, the other molding one of her breasts, pulling on her taut, stiff nipple.

Alone, with no one around, no one to disturb her, no one to make demands on her, she felt free to fondle and pleasure herself as no one else could.

In a way that she *allowed* no one else to do.

Her toying fingers picked up in speed and depth as she plunged them inside her vagina, rotating them, seeking out her inner spot. Once found, she soon felt the tingling sensation that signaled her body was ready to release.

She moaned softly while her body jerked and spasmed when her orgasm took over her body. As her body clenched one final time, she bit her bottom lip to prevent the cry from escalating, panting, taking in deep breaths of air as she finished the climax.

Once her body had calmed, she withdrew her shaky fingers, turned on the gold-tinted faucet taps, and quickly washed her hands.

She saw the deep flush that ran beneath her dark-brown skin and a fine line of sweat bead her brow as she stared at her reflection in the gold-tinted mirror.

Despite the sexual euphoria that enveloped her after her self-given orgasm, Chase felt completely unfulfilled.

Walking toward the bedroom, she quickly unpacked her clothes, carefully hanging the garments inside the ornately carved armoire. Pulling out a colorful sarong, she dressed and took a tour around the cottage, familiarizing herself with her temporary digs.

Feeling anxious, she picked up the phone and called for her attendant, deciding to attend the luau. It was that or go insane as she waited for her *fantasy* to begin.

CHAPTER 7

"Is everything to your satisfaction, Miss?"

Chastity turned from the large bay window where she'd been admiring the view of the moon rising, casting a surreal golden glow over the nearby ocean.

She was startled when she heard the voice behind her speak. She turned to see her guide standing in the doorway of her bedroom.

He'd brought her home from the luau over thirty minutes ago. She'd immediately stripped out her clothes, taken a brisk shower, and had slipped on a long, sheer nightgown, with the intent of sliding into the luxurious, king-sized bed that dominated her temporary bedroom and going to sleep.

"It's beautiful," she replied simply, and turned back around, continuing to admire the scene.

"I'm glad you find your accommodations to your pleasure, Ms. Davidson. However, it's time to go."

"Excuse me?"

"I said, it's time to go. Please come with me." His voice remained pleasant, yet his tone brooked no argument. His tone and his wording raised the hair on the back of her neck.

He walked further into her bedroom, stopping when he

stood several feet away from her. There were no lights on in the cottage, the only illumination came from the glowing moon. Feeling exposed, Chase wrapped her arms around herself.

"Time to go where?" Her forehead creased as she asked the question.

"What you came here for, Ms. Davidson. Your fantasy begins now." His voice didn't rise, and there was little inflection in his tone. Yet, it disturbed her.

He advanced closer. The small, reassuring smile he gave didn't give her any comfort; instead, she felt a sense of anxiety. An odd fear threatened to overwhelm her.

"Let me get dressed. I just stepped out of the shower," she replied after a heartbeat of silence. She motioned a hand over her body, indicating her state of dress.

When she moved to turn away, his hand on her arm stilled her.

"No. It's time now. What you're wearing doesn't matter."

"Look. I said—"

"Now, Ms. Davidson. I believe you have a pair of shoes at the entryway? You can put them on, on our way out."

Although his pleasant smile remained fixed, he directed just a bit more force on her wrist, not enough to hurt, but enough that she felt the added pressure.

"You wouldn't want them to go on without you, would you, Ms. Davidson? You wouldn't want to prolong a moment longer, your desire to be number one?"

They stared at each other and in Chase's mind images of Javier's mocking smile flashed through her mind.

"Don't you want to receive what you deserve?"

She straightened her back, drew in her chest and with one

hand, easily removed the man's hold on her wrist. "Yes. I'm ready."

Ignoring his edict that she not change, Chase grabbed the long, decorative fabric—one of many pieces she'd bought from the small gift store after she'd left the luau—off a chair and wrapped it securely around her body, tying the ends in a knot above her breasts.

With that she followed him, stopping to slip on her strappy sandals before leaving the cottage. She closed the door behind her, and a small grin lifted the corners of her mouth, anticipation replacing the earlier unwanted fear.

"You mentioned they were all waiting for me. I don't suppose you can tell me what that means?" she asked, doubting the silent man would enlighten her. "And what is your name? I don't think you've ever told me," she said, not knowing if he'd told her and she'd simply not paid attention, or if had never given it.

"My name is Gideon. But, as to the rest of your question, I'm afraid I am not at liberty to give you any information regarding the upcoming events. You'll know soon enough," he replied. Chase was a bit taken aback with his response.

She came out of the house expecting to see the white Jeep he'd driven or at least some type of island-motorized vehicle, but she saw none. She lifted a brow in question when he held her elbow, tugged her along with him, and began to walk along the bushy trail that ran alongside her cottage.

Pushing aside the heavy, abundant foliage in front of them, he cleared a path for her as he walked ahead. Chase was glad she'd wrapped the fabric around her body, saving it from any scratches the branches and foliage would have given her. Thankfully, the ground beneath her was soft. Beneath the delicate soles of her sandals, she couldn't feel sand or rocks, nothing but the soft bed of leaves and grass that carpeted the tropical flooring.

The light from the moon seemed to be the main illumination the further they walked, leaving behind the distant lights from other parts of the resorts that shone brightly near her cottage. Chase glanced behind her in growing concern at the fading lights of the resort the farther they walked along the path.

"How much farther?" Irritably she batted away a low-hanging leafy branch as she continued to follow him. She felt as though she'd been walking for miles, and she saw no end in sight.

The earlier feeling of anticipation began to fade away; trepidation and uncertainty took its place.

It was then the low murmur of a multitude of voices, their hushed tones carrying on the wind, reached her ears.

It was also at that moment that Gideon stepped out into an open stretch of beach. He moved aside and pointed a finger in the direction in front of them.

Further up the beach, near the edge of the shore, was what looked to be a large gathering of people, all seated in front of a raised platform. As soon as she moved around him, a hundred or more heads turned. She suppressed a shiver despite the humid temperature when even in the dark she felt the hungry, lustful stares of a hundred pair of eyes boring into her.

"Please, come forward, Chase. We've been waiting for you," a loud masculine voice invited her. Chase's eyes left the hungry-eyed crowd and sought out the one who spoke.

A man stood on the platform with a microphone in his hand, dressed formally in the tropical paradise, wearing a dark tuxedo, widely smiling at her, holding out a hand, inviting her to join him on the wooden dais.

Her breathing increased, her heart beat out strong staccato thumps against her breasts as Chase allowed Gideon to guide her toward the waiting crowd.

CHAPTER 8

"You're leaving?" Chase asked, turning to the only familiar face in her uncertain world. She felt an almost desperate desire to beg him to stay, to not leave her alone.

"Yes, this is where I leave you on your journey, Ms. Davidson."

"Wha—what do you mean?"

"I have to." She saw a look of sadness enter his eyes as though he wished he did not have to do so. "But you will be in capable hands. I must leave you now to your auctioneer."

"My auctioneer?" Her voice had risen and carried on the wind, seeming to magnify it.

Her head whipped around so swiftly that several strands of hair loosened from the careful topknot she'd created on top of her head, and fell into her eyes. She stared first at the waiting man on the stage, then her gaze went to those who sat in folded chairs in the audience, openly staring…gawking at her.

Her lips partially opened, and her tongue swiped across her now-dry lips. When she turned back to Gideon, it was to find him gone. He'd blended into the darkness as though he was never there.

"Please, come. Join us, Ms. Davidson."

Chase turned reluctantly to face the crowd and the smiling

man on the stage. Swallowing a melon ball-sized lump of fear, she forced her feet to move, slowly walking toward the stage.

She kept her gaze averted from the avid crowd, not ready to face them, unsure of their role in all of this.

As she made the short journey toward the stage, she stared in fascination at the assortment of large, life-sized tiki wooden carvings lining the walkway, some easily depicting males and females, some odd caricatures of both.

When she heard a drum begin to beat, she turned her head toward the sound. Directly in front of her a bare-chested man covered in tribal-looking tattoos over his upper torso, an ornate mask covering the upper half of his face, his long, dark hair flowing down his back, strummed a steady harsh rhythm on the large drum gripped between his thick, muscled thighs.

The closer she drew to the stage, the heavier the beat of his drum.

Chase felt a fine sheen of perspiration trickle down the side of her face.

Once she reached the stage, she grasped the man's opened hand. Solicitously, he helped her up the short flight of stairs that led to the stage.

"She's here, the one we've all been waiting for, the one you all have been eagerly waiting for. Isn't she beautiful?"

The smile he gave her was encouraging, before he gave his attention back to the eager crowd, tugging a bewildered Chase along with him.

"Don't be shy, Ms. Davidson. Come forth and allow them all to see you!"

"I'm not sure this is what I requested." She spoke so low that she doubted the grinning man could hear her. Doubt mingled with trepidation, churning maliciously in her gut. She cast nervous eyes over the murmuring audience.

Again he smiled that strange predatory smile that brought absurd images of Little Red Riding Hood and the wolf to mind.

Chase straightened her back, forcibly bringing herself back in tight control and reining in her fear.

She was no wilting Little Red Riding Hood. She wasn't afraid of the Big Bad Wolf.

"No one is going to bite. At least, not unless you ask them to," he replied, loudly enough for everyone to hear. Despite the loud music and excited crowd, he obviously heard her.

At his quip, she heard a mixture of rumbling male amusement and tinkling feminine laughter.

She turned toward the audience, her eyes sweeping over them. She had to squint her eyes to see them against the beaming lights that circled the stage. On the beach she'd been able to see their faces more clearly. However, now on the stage, with the surrounding tiki lights, all shining down and focused on her, she was unable to see individual people. The bodies and faces in the crowd merged into one homogenous blob.

"We are ready for the final bidding this evening," the man—the auctioneer—began. Bewildered, Chase turned to him, her eyes widening.

"The *what?*"

He ignored her and continued, "What you have all been waiting all evening for, the piece de resistance, I present to you, Chastity Davidson. Ms. Davidson is a prime specimen, isn't she? Look at her, beautiful, intelligent…and talented. For the one who dares to bid on her, untold nights of pleasure will sure to be yours from this dark beauty," he finished with a flourish, stroking a hand down the length of her body, his strokes feather light.

"I don't know what's going on here, but I'm not staying around to find out!" Chase's heart began to pound frantically against her ribcage, as she shoved his hands away from her body. She spun around, her desire to leave paramount, when she tripped and would have gone sprawling off the stage, had he not grabbed her by the arm to prevent her fall.

He brought her up, close to his chest, his dark eyes boring into hers. His stare was so hot, so intense that it seemed to sear a direct path into her soul.

"Isn't this what you wanted, your deepest desire, to be number one?"

"Yes! But not like this!" Chase hissed.

He leaned closer, his warm breath scorching the back of her neck.

She flinched when she felt his lips feather against her neck in a fleeting kiss.

"No?"

The muscles in her jaw tensed. She clenched her teeth so hard together they ached. She moved her head to the side, her breathing harsh, and her face flushed, refusing to look at him.

He placed his hands on her shoulders, forcing her to turn and face the crowd.

"Can't you feel their energy, their excitement?" he whispered against the side of her face, for her ears alone.

Her nostrils flared, her chest rose heavily as her gaze was helplessly, almost against her will, drawn to the nearly invisible faces of the crowd.

"Their desire…it's all for you. And you alone. Only you can appease them."

Chase swallowed deeply.

Although she couldn't see them clearly, she *felt* them. Their lust and sexual energy shot through her body, infusing her with their collective ardor.

The auctioneer's hands slowly moved down her shoulders and over her breasts.

"Only you can satisfy their longings."

She scarcely noticed when he deftly unknotted the ties of the fabric and the cloth fell from her body, leaving her body starkly outlined in the sheer dress.

She felt the crowd's randy anticipation, their excitement.

"They've been waiting for you and you alone, Chastity."

Their lust was a palpable living entity—one so tangible she felt its shadowy, invisible fingers move insidiously down her spine, curl over her body, her breasts, her stomach, and stroke her between her thighs.

Distantly, she felt his hands roam over her body as she stared out, in odd fascination, over the excited crowd.

"Would you deny them the opportunity to make you number one?" he murmured.

The fingers of their combined lust stroked her just as the auctioneer stroked her in a symphonic rhythm. The heavy beat of the drum began to pulse in time with the hammering beat of the walls in her pussy.

She heard the auctioneer lightly chuckle, as though he *knew*...

He continued to skim his hands over her body. He bunched her gown in his fist and slid it up her legs, past her waist, exposing her.

"Who among you is able to tame this beauty? Who can crash through her walls, break down her barriers to reach the hidden treasures she keeps so carefully locked away?"

His words seemed to come from a small distance. She heard them, yet they didn't register in her mind, she was so caught up in the surreal nature of what was happening to her.

He gently pressed a finger into her creaming pussy, adding a second finger while his thumb feathered across her pulsing clit, spreading her own cream around the extended nub.

"Hmmm," he murmured. "So hot." He closed his eyes briefly after bringing the evidence of her arousal to his nostrils and inhaled deeply.

He took his finger into his mouth, licked her cum away, and smiled. "So sweet."

It all felt like a dream to her as she turned her head slightly and watched dispassionately as he licked his finger and smiled.

The air around her grew thick, hotter. Dewy beads of moisture trickled between her breasts.

"Who among you is man...or woman...enough to take on the challenge she lays before you?"

He grabbed the top of her dress and ripped it apart, exposing her fully to the now frantic crowd.

Lifting one heavy breast, he palmed as much as his hand would hold, thumbing a finger over her tight, spiked nipple.

"Who is ready to start bidding on this nubile Amazon?" he laughingly called out.

The crowd began to jump to its feet in a frenzy of sexual energy.

"Are you ready to be number one, Chase?"

The auctioneer's gaze settled on her, his eyes were hot blazing beams of sexual tension.

Nothing about what he was saying, what he was doing, should have appealed to her.

His look, his touch—none of that should have affected her except for disgust and loathing.

Yet, as she stared into his hard, unyielding gaze, it did. *He* did.

She turned to the animated crowd.

They did.

Their frenzy, desire, franticness...It all called to her, called to everything in her that longed to yield.

To give in.

But not just to give in for their bidding.

She turned back to him, seeing the challenge in his dark eyes.

"Who among you is man or woman enough to break her down? To conquer her?"

As her gaze locked with the auctioneer, a delicious, forbidden desire to succumb to the utter madness of the auction rocked her very being.

She turned around, struck out her breasts and dislodged his hands from her body.

She closed her eyes, tilted her head to the side. As her tongue darted out of her mouth to moisten her lips, she boldly ran her hands down her body. With no apology, she showed off her body to those who *thought* they'd be the *one*; the one to break her.

She opened her eyes. raised one single brow at the auctioneer and stepped away from him.

A low laugh tumbled from her lips as she faced the bidding crowd.

The adrenaline coursed fiercely through Chase's veins. Every nerve ending was tingling with anticipation, and the high from the bidding heightened with every call outbidding the last.

She stood before them all, proudly resplendent in her nakedness. She had attended several auctions, but never in her wildest imagination had she ever envisioned the likes of this one. The sheer forbidden quality of it damn near made her giddy, as her head whipped over the crowd, the bids reaching astronomical levels, as each one quickly outbid the other, the bids fast, staccato, hitting hard.

"Five million," a feminine voice rang loudly over the bidding crowd.

A hush fell over the crowd, stilling all action.

Chase squinted against the glare clouding her vision, trying to see who had called out the incredulous amount, but was unable to locate the lone woman.

Her heart thud erratically against her chest, her body drenched with sweat as though she'd just completed a ten mile full out run as she scanned the crowd, wondering just as all the others, if anyone would—could—top the bid.

She turned toward the auctioneer. He held out a hand for her to take.

With her hand trembling, she placed it within his.

"I believe we have—"

Before the auctioneer could end the bidding and declare a winning bid, a deep baritone cut in.

"Twenty-five million."

The crowd's murmuring reached even higher decimals as heads turned in the direction of the voice.

The auctioneer smiled, nodding his head in deference to the direction of the voice.

"I believe we have a winner," he replied simply.

CHAPTER 9

Immediately after the last astonishing bid, Gideon appeared onstage, and Chase was whisked away before she could process all that had transpired. She barely had enough time to gather her ruined garments and re-clothe herself with the torn clothing.

Instead of walking back to her bungalow, as she'd expected, he placed her in the familiar white Jeep, and within minutes they'd arrived back to her temporary home.

Now, with a cigarette clamped between her lips, Chase paced the length of her living area, occasionally walking toward the front door that she'd left opened to peer into the darkness.

She stepped out onto the small porch, one eye narrowing against the curling smoke from the cigarette, searching for signs of someone coming.

"So let the games begin already," she muttered irritably.

She inhaled deeply on the cigarette, holding the smoke deep inside for a moment before blowing it out in a gush of air.

With disgust, she raised a slightly shaky hand to her lips and snatched the half-smoked cigarette out of her mouth and threw it on the ground, stubbing out the burning ember with the heel of her sandal.

She stalked back inside, kicked off her shoes, and slammed the door shut.

Striding through the cottage, she went into the bedroom and stripped off the new fabric wrap she'd worn after returning from the auction. She lay down on the bed, staring up at the ceiling.

Waiting.

Her body was alive and humming in eager anticipation, although what was in store for her, what eroticism she would experience as the night wore on, was an uncertainty.

"Just what in hell I'm waiting for I don't have a damn clue."

As she lay on the bed, she raised a naked arm and noted the fine trembling of her hands as she stared down at it.

Just like a junkie, she was coming down from the high of the auction.

The rush of adrenaline that had pumped through her veins was finally wearing off. Just like any other junkie, she was primed for the next fix.

Frantic for the next high.

But like any good high, this one not only had her jonesing for the next fix, but it had worn her out—so much so that when she closed her eyes, she fell into a restless sleep.

CHAPTER 10

Quietly and with as much stealth as a seasoned cat burglar, Chastity carefully opened, then eased her long legs through her bedroom window. She manipulated and contorted her body to get inside.

She closed the window shut and lightly jumped down into her room, landing with a soft thud on the hardwood floors.

Just as she turned, she bumped against the small nightstand table and bit back a curse.

She quickly righted the stand before it could fall to the floor, afraid the sound would alert her mother that she wasn't in her bed, on the off chance that Maybelle had made it home from work before Chase. There was little chance of that because she hadn't seen Maybelle's beat-up Chevy in the driveway, yet she still remained as quiet as possible.

Chase glanced down at the brightly illuminated dial on her watch.

She had at least an hour before Maybelle would be home from her late-night shift at the nursing home. More than enough time to shower, get dressed, jump into bed, and not risk getting busted for being out.

She quickly shed her clothing and opened a bureau drawer to withdraw her night clothes. Carefully closing the door, she turned around, and blinked her eyes several times when the bright overhead lights in her bedroom came on.

Chastity's heart fell to her stomach when she came face to face with her mother as she stood in her doorway.

"You may as well stop trying to pretend. I know your ass has been out. I got home early from work. Hid the car 'round back."

In her hands, Maybelle held two long strips of leather, slapping them against each other.

Chastity nearly passed out in fear.

"Bet you didn't think that was gonna happen, did you? Imagine my surprise when you weren't here, where you were supposed to be. I told you to stay home, Chastity. And you had to disobey. Now, you goin' to have to pay."

Chastity clutched the gown she held in one hand, the other held out in entreaty, as though to ward off Maybelle. "But, Momma, I *had* to go to the library. I had to finish my report for school. I—"

"*Shut up*! *I* told you to stay your ass at home."

Maybelle pushed away from the doorframe, walking further inside and casting narrowed eyes around the neat room.

Chastity bit her lip as her mother inspected the room, her eyes following the motion of the leather strips being slapped against Maybelle's stubby, fat hands. She sent a prayer heavenward that was nothing out of order in her room.

"As though I believe you were at the library studying," Maybelle scoffed. Grunting, she lowered her round body to the floor to peer beneath Chastity's bed.

Slowly, she backed away from her mother. "I…I was! I won't get credit if I don't turn in the report," Chastity cried out.

Maybelle whipped her head around from beneath the bed and put a hand out to brace herself as she rose. She pinned

Chastity with a glare. "I said shut the fuck up! I know you were out with some boy, you tramp. Don't lie to me!"

As her mother advanced on her with an evil and crazy glint in her eyes focused directly on her, Chastity slowly backed away until the back of her knees hit the edge of her bed.

"You think you can sneak out of here when I'm hard at work, trying to put food on the goddamn table and a roof over your ungrateful head?" Maybelle yelled. "I know you were out, probably screwing some boy. Stop lying to me, goddamn it!"

Before she could make a run for it, Maybelle grabbed her with a speed and strength that defied the physical limitations of her short, rotund body. She yanked Chastity close and flipped her around, pulling her arms behind her back. Within seconds she had secured the leather straps in her hands around Chastity's wrists.

She shoved Chastity down to the bed, and quickly secured her feet, wrapping the second leather cord around them and secured each ankle to the other before looping the cord around the footboard of the bed.

"No! Don't do this to me, Momma…please!" Chase screamed, tears running down her face as she bucked against the tight restraints.

After she'd secured Chastity to the bed, Maybelle moved away and laughed, her dark face flushed and her large breasts heaving with the exertion.

"Maybe your fast ass will think twice about sneaking out after this!"

"Momma…please! Don't leave me like this! Please, don't let… him." She stopped and swallowed, before choking out in a whisper, "Don't let Daddy come…come," she begged.

Her pleading cries fell on deaf ears.

"He seems to be the only person your lying ass obeys," she replied.

With a look of disgust, Maybelle spun around, shut off the lights and slammed the door shut, leaving Chastity alone, shivering.

She stared at the mocking shadows in the dark, cold room, waiting.

She fell asleep, despite her intent not to, wakening with a cry on her lips when a heavy, putrid-smelling body pressed her into the coarse sheets on her small twin bed.

Chase fought against the dream, fought against the binds that held her as she lay on her small bed, tossing her head back and forth on the pillow as her body bucked against the tight restraints her mother had placed over her limbs.

"Please, Momma…don't leave me like this! I'll be good, I promise!" she cried, tears streaming down her face.

When she felt cool, soft lips fasten over hers and a warm tongue ease between the seams of her lips, she moaned as she fought her attacker, determined that she wouldn't let him do it again.

She would rather die than allow her father to force himself on her again.

When she felt hands stroking up her thighs, a hard body snaking up the length of her body, a pair of hands stroking a hot caress along her instep, her eyes snapped open.

She struggled against the drugging kisses and dregs of the nightmare that held her an unwilling captive.

She forced her head away and shoved against the hands, tongues, and fingers that ran over her body.

Struggling to sit up, she tried to push the body that covered hers away and found that her wrists were clamped together by a pair of strong hands, pinning them above her head.

"What the hell is this?" She choked out the words, shaking off the last sediment of the long-ago nightmare as she fought her unknown assailant.

She saw nothing more than the shadowy imprint of bodies in the midnight darkness of the room, blanketing her body, pressing her into the silk sheets of the bed.

"Sssh, it's okay, just—"

"Hell no, it's not okay! Get the hell off of me! All of you!" Chase interrupted, renewing her struggles to free herself from the restraining hold and the hot bodies that covered and stroked her naked body.

She raised her body and snatched her hands from the tight, masculine hands that held her. Although she could see nothing in the unnaturally dark room, she swung her hand in a wild arc. Satisfaction coursed through her body when she heard the satisfying crack of her hand meeting flesh.

When she felt hands on the opposite end of her body grab her thighs, she pulled her legs up and kicked out.

"Fuck!" she cursed when she missed her intended target.

Her legs were grabbed and held at the same moment that her body was slammed back to the mattress, knocking the wind out of her and stunning her for a moment.

It was enough time for one of her attackers to regain hold of her wrists.

"That's what we're trying to do," a second voice bit the words out. Seconds later she heard a discernible click and felt cold, steel handcuffs lock into place.

Her bound wrists were manacled to one of the wrought-iron poles of the headboard.

The same mouth that brought her out of sleep, again slanted over hers, pushing against her lips to slide a tongue deep inside.

This time she was awake and aware, not caught in the dream world of sleep, not some helpless little girl who had to submit to the tyranny of someone bigger and stronger than her.

She bit the lip kissing her. As the assailant broke the kiss with a curse, she felt the coppery feel of blood fill her mouth.

"He said she wouldn't be easy to conquer," someone said, the voice coming from the lower end of the bed.

He? Who were they talking about? Chase wondered. *God, what was this madness?*

"At twenty-five mil, hope it's worth the price to find out," a silky voice murmured, his voice coming from the side of the bed. Chase realized that there were at least three men in the dark room, all trying to conquer her.

"Whoever the hell *he* is...he was right," Chase spoke behind clenched teeth. "And I should have known."

"You should have known?" the one nearest to her, the one who'd awakened and assaulted her without her permission, spoke.

"That it would take more than one to answer the challenge," she scoffed. "That it took three of you to pool your money... and your dicks...together to win."

A finger reached out and stroked down her cheek, down her throat and onward, caressing down the line of her cleavage. A large hand cupped one of her breasts, thumbing a callused finger over her nipple. Despite her anger, her body reacted, her nipples beading and seeking the rough caress.

"Ah, that's where you're wrong. We're simply one of your appetizers," he said and stopped talking.

She felt his slick, long tongue snake the same path his fingers had—down her throat, licking a hot path to the crest of one breast, tugging the nipple into his mouth, while the fingers of his other hand palmed and caressed the other heavy orb. He clamped his warm mouth over the upper swell of her breast, pulling and sucking her nipple until it spiked hard and tight.

"You're not ready for the main meal, yet," he murmured after releasing her breast and moving away.

"What...what are you talking—" Her stumbling was cut off mid-question when she felt a balmy breath blow across her sex, followed by a tongue stroking deep into her cunt.

Her body arched sharply off the mattress, and Chase bit back a moan. Her cream eased from her pussy despite her resistance. Wet kisses scored down her inner leg, licking over her knees, and down her leg, lightly grasping one of her feet.

She struggled against the invasion. Her nails scored deep grooves into her palms as she clenched her fists, unsuccessfully trying to escape the bonds that held her hands securely in place.

With a strangled breath, she struggled against the deceptively soft kisses, refusing to give in to her body's demands and the sexual lethargy that threatened to overwhelm her.

"How do you feel?" a deep, husky voice asked, jerking her away from the sensations flooding her body and the internal fight she was having with her mind and body.

She gasped when she felt the man blanketing her back reach across her body and scrape his thumb against her clit.

"I...it feels...good." The admission was torn from her tightly clenched lips.

The hand playing with her clit moved, and she felt a firm-stinging slap to her backside, followed by him running his hand over the stinging flesh to ease the sting.

She gasped, tugging against the restraints with renewed fervor.

"No. You didn't answer the question. How do *you* feel?"

"Out of control." The admission filled her with shame.

When nubile fingers separated the lips of her vagina and a finger caressed the flesh between the dripping folds, Chase growled from deep within her throat.

She heard a myriad of satisfied murmurs at her response.

"We've just begun," one of the deep, husky voices replied.

Her lips were captured again, in a hot, nasty kiss that set her body tingling. "You need to succumb, Chastity. You need to give in to the pleasure. Stop trying to exert your will. The sooner you do so, the sooner you'll be ready for him."

"Him? Who...what are you talking about?"

In the dark, she sought out the man's gaze but was given no time to consider his words before he was on her again, before they all converged back on her with a myriad of tongues, lips, teeth, and hands.

She moved, seeking out the firm yet sensually soft lips of the one kissing her.

The man drank deeply from her; his hands stroked the smooth fleshy mounds of her ass, and another set caressed and fondled her body in a series of nips, licks, and kisses, all of which brought Chase to a feverish pitch of wanton desire. She was drunk with lust, her body on fire.

A slick tongue parted her lips and pressed hotly inside, pushing past her teeth to ravage her mouth, devouring her in hot strokes and darting away before Chase's tongue could capture his.

His lips captured the lower rim of her lip and bit; the sting caused a sharp zing directly to her pussy.

Simultaneously, she felt strong, masculine hands press her thighs apart, while a rock-hard chest hovered behind her pressing insistently against her back.

God, how many of them are there? Chase thought, her mind in a sexual fog of lust and desire.

Long, lean fingers grasped her breasts, palming and toying with the orbs before tugging on her spiked nipples.

Her nipples tightened painfully, elongating, begging for more attention.

Hands lifted her, rolling her body until she was lying on her side, all done without any break in contact; the multiple hands continued to stroke, pet and caress her.

"Lift your body," a deep voice, different than one kissing her, commanded, and Chase obeyed. A soft pillow eased between her and the mattress, cushioning and raising her hips.

Her outer leg was raised, and her big toe slid past a set of full lips before being engulfed in a warm mouth that pulled on the toe and suckled it deeply. Chase whimpered against the lips slashing over hers.

There was a deep answering laugh, and her toe was released. That tongue now trailed a path from her foot up her legs before landing between her thighs.

She felt a shift; bodies moved on hers in an easy exchange, and the face between her legs settled between her thighs. When a slick tongue flicked out, capturing her blood-turgid clit, she cried out.

His fingers quickly joined his tongue, in a symphony of moves that soon had Chase bucking against his face, her moans now loud and harsh in the dark room.

The man kissing her mouth pulled away, and Chase leaned forward to try and recapture the connection, angry when the bonds restricted her from doing so.

Her body and mind strained against the onslaught of sensations. She grew restless, her skin felt too tight, and her breath came out in strangled gasps when suddenly the broad, fleshy knob of a penis pressed insistently against her lips with a silent but obvious command for her to open.

She opened her mouth wide and allowed him to feed her his shaft slowly until the tip bumped the back of her throat.

Her tongue hollowed. She cupped the soft, slick underside of the silky skin of his dick, wrapping her tongue around it and stroking from side to side before curling her tongue over the top of his cock, repeating the same careful movements.

She felt his hands on each side of her face, the rough pads of twin thumbs softly stroking her cheeks as her head bobbed up and down on his shaft. He withdrew from her in small increments. Chase followed his lead, licking her way to the top of his dick, circling the thick ridge around the knob and greedily lapping the drip of pre-cum away from the tiny eye in the center before deep-throating him again.

She felt hands on her hips, smoothly moving her to lay on her side. As she was moved, she never lost connection with the stiff rod in her mouth or the tongue suckling deeply into her cunt. The cheeks of her buttocks were gently spread, and a body settled behind her.

Feeling overwhelmed, she began to fight against the onslaught of sensation; squirming against the restraints that held her hands immobile and the strong hands that securely held the rest of her body firmly in place.

Seconds later a hot tongue slid around the puckered hole of her anus, flickering in short, tight swirls against her before easing inside, along with a long index finger. Her heart pounded against her chest and despite the cool fan swirling a breeze over her naked flesh, Chase was unbearably hot. A pool of sweat eased down her face, between her breasts, and the cream from her pussy gushed down her leg. She grunted against the cock in her mouth in sensual agony when a tongue joined the finger playing against her puckered hole.

Her skin felt as though it were wrapped in flames.

When a small pencil-thin object replaced the finger and tongue stroking her, and a cool gel filled deep inside, she inhaled a sharp breath. She hissed in painful pleasure when oily fingers rubbed more of the gel over and around her puckered hole, before pressing deeply into her ass.

Seconds later, a thick, hot cock took the place of fingers and began to work slowly into her ass. The pressure was intense despite the lubricant and Chase moaned around the cock in her mouth. The pressure continued to build, and she helplessly released a scream as the multitude of sensations rained down on her.

Every part of her body was being suckled…laved…fucked. When the man between her thighs reached a hand up and began to fondle her breasts, Chase drew in a deep breath before slowly releasing the pent-up hair in a harsh whimper.

Moaning, mentally she fought against her own body's reaction, fought against the pleasure being forced on her. Yet, she continued to undulate her hips against the dual invasion below and suckle the cock in her mouth.

Her body now had a mind of its own. No longer was she in control of it.

She moaned even as she accepted the strokes and thrusts—pussy, breasts, ass—every part of her was being catered to, propelling her to a fevered pitch of mindless lust.

Sliding back and forth, her ass sought the pleasure of the dick plunging deep inside her buttocks. Her thighs were shaking, quivering around the head between her legs as a fevered tongue continued to stroke and suckle her cunt. The sound of a multitude of harsh breaths and moans of delights combined into one melodious song of rapture.

When Chase felt the orgasm slamming into her, she fought against it.

She ripped her mouth away, twisting and bucking her body against the dual invasion of pussy and ass. She was unable to stop the incredulous orgasm that threatened to break her, she screamed as she released.

Her body bowed down on itself as the orgasm washed over her as violent as a tsunami and just as devastating.

As her orgasm reached its pinnacle, a strange feeling enveloped her, one she'd never felt. Her body tingled, and a queasy, disorienting feeling swamped her.

Damn. She was going to faint. The reality hit her, stunning her.

Before losing consciousness, she felt hot cum splash against her body in a multitude of jetting streams.

Down her face, running down her chin, its sticky path ran between her breasts.

Over the rounded cheek of her ass, it slowly, slowly trickled down her body. Against her mound, it ran in hot streams, mingling with her own cum.

Coating, marking, claiming her.

Dominating her.

Chase gasped when she was harshly awakened when a slender but long cock pressed deep into her ass while a thick shaft pushed into her vagina.

Her stomach clenched as the burning pressure she felt on both ends tore through her. Panting, her eyes fluttered open.

She had only passed out for mere moments, but it was enough time for the men to reposition her and remove the bonds.

In the midnight darkness of the room, she was barely able to see a man whose strong muscled ass was near her face, his body bracketing her upper torso. Yet she felt his long dick tap against her lips, silently demanding that she open, again.

Flat on her back, with her legs bent, raised and spread, two men were steadily pumping into her, fucking her to full wakefulness—one in her pussy. the other stroking deep into her ass.

The one straddling her face with his shaft at her lips was perched with his head at the top of her mound, his wicked tongue flicking against her clit.

Moaning, she spread her legs further apart and opened her lips to allow him to ease his rod deep into her mouth. She swallowed it deeply.

In a smooth rhythm, her head bobbed up and down on his shaft, sliding it nearly out of her mouth before she swallowed him again.

Oh God, what am I doing? Chase thought as she milked his cock of the sweet cum that eased down her throat.

She was caught in some type of mad dream. A dream where her body and mind were no longer hers to command as she eagerly lapped her tongue around him, swallowing his cum even as her hips began to undulate, meeting, matching, and eagerly greeting the powerful thrusts of each man between her legs.

She rolled her hips against the dual invasion below, even as her mouth fastened hungrily on the cock in her mouth, her teeth lightly scraping the soft underskin of his shaft, her tongue delicately fondling the twin plum-like testicles.

Chase willingly let go of thoughts about what was right, what was wrong, who was in control…None of that mattered in that moment.

Instead, she fully participated in the wild loving.

CHAPTER 11

Chase opened her eyes and blinked her eyes rapidly against the bright glare of the sun that shafted through the sheer, ivory-colored curtains.

The curtains softly swayed as the early morning, warm breeze wafted past them to whisper over her, cooling her naked skin.

She slowly eased her sore body into a sitting position and turned again to gaze at the billowing curtains, idly wondering when the window had been opened. She glanced down at her body, cringing when she saw the evidence of last night's excess on her dark-brown skin.

She ran her fingers over her breasts and down her stomach. Her fingers came away sticky as she removed the remnants of white cum that was plastered to her skin like glue.

After the first time, they had continued to fuck her, long into the night, even when she thought no other response could be wrung from her, when she thought her body was exhausted, beyond satiated…

Chase winced, ashamed of what she'd allowed to happen.

She gave in to every one of their demands, as they stroked, licked, and fucked every part of her body, finding places on her she hadn't known were hot spots, to bring her to a screaming climax long through the night and into the early morning hours.

With only token protests from her initially, they managed to break her down, had conquered her.

"Damn," she whispered.

They had broken down her physical barriers, and had her accepting...

"Shit, who am I kidding? They had me begging for it." She sighed, blowing a breath that fanned the curls of hair lying limply against her cheek.

She threw her legs over the edge of the bed to get up and hissed when the muscles in her legs screamed out in protest, shaking and failing, due to the extreme and unnatural positions her body had been placed in throughout most of the night.

Bending her sore body to pick up the wrap that lay in a heap on the floor near the bed, Chase tied the ends over her breasts and padded barefoot into the adjoining bathroom.

She stared at herself in the smoky-glass-tinted mirror, seeing the dark rings under her eyes and her hair that curled wildly. She fingered the curls that lay in a sweaty riot over her head, long ago sweated out from their original flat-iron straightness.

"God, I'm a mess," she mumbled, pulling her hair back tightly with one hand while searching with the other hand for something to hold it, before she allowed her hands to drop.

She laughed, lightening her dark mood, and left her hair alone.

Here she was thinking about her hair when she'd just had one of the most out-of-control sexual experiences of her life.

Turning away, she walked the short distance to the shower and turned the knobs to the far left to allow hot water to come pouring from the jets before stepping inside.

She leisurely washed. Carefully, she soaped between her legs, gently separating her vaginal lips, wincing when her fingers touched the still-tender flesh. She turned her face fully into the stinging overhead spray, scrubbing her face, body, and hair… She futilely attempted to scrub away the memory of what she'd done the night before, shying away from delving too deeply into her thoughts on what she'd fully participated in.

After the shower, she donned a two-piece swimsuit and again wrapped the fabric around herself, securely it around her hips—this time, fashioning a skirt.

Walking out of the bedroom, she was hit with a delicious, aromatic smell wafting from the kitchen. Curious, she walked over and saw several dome-covered platters on the counter.

Lifting one of the lids, she discovered an array of breakfast delicacies of thinly sliced ham, fat little sausages, petit croissants, and an assortment of fruits.

Just as with the window, someone had come into her cottage without her knowledge, anticipating her needs in a way that she found uncomfortable.

Although her stomach growled, and the food looked amazing, she found the thought of eating unappealing and instead lifted the small carafe of coffee to pour into one of the mugs set out for her use. Then she caught sight of a second carafe alongside a wine goblet.

Curious, she poured from the second carafe and took a careful sip before realizing it was a mimosa. The sweet juice had been spiked with enough champagne that she'd easily discerned its taste.

After last night, she needed something much stronger than caffeine.

She drank the glass in one long, thirsty gulp, and placed the goblet down on the counter. She poured another glass, carrying it with her through the kitchen and staring out the opened windows to the welcoming, deserted beach below.

She walked toward the living area and grabbed the chenille blanket casually placed over the arm of a corner chair and tossed it over her shoulder, then walked back into the kitchen.

Donning the sandals she left near the entry, Chase decided to walk to the beach before it became populated with any other island guests. She needed the tranquility and peace that came only when she could be completely alone.

A time she desperately needed to come to grips with the wild curveballs life had thrown her over the last few days.

"Beautiful morning, isn't it?"

Startled, Chase jumped and twisted her upper body around as a deep, melodic voice intruded her solitary thoughts.

"Yes, it is," she murmured in response and glanced up.

She brought her hand to her forehead to shield the blazing sun from her eyes, wishing she'd thought to bring her sunglasses to the beach. She inhaled a swift breath.

She stared up into the face of one of the most beautiful men she'd ever seen.

His skin, the color of smooth, rich cream, was flawless. She ran her eyes over the perfect symmetry of his features: his deeply set, gray eyes; sharply cut cheekbones; bold, aquiline nose, and full, sensual lips—lips that were perfectly sculpted. Lips made for sin.

Taken separately, his features were bold, aristocratic, and at odds with one another. But together, they fit, beautifully so, as though a master artesian had, with careful precision, sculpted each one.

It was him.

The man who'd been watching her so intently at the welcome luau she'd attended upon arriving at the island.

When she'd been invited to attend the luau she'd gone, knowing good and well that if she stayed in her cottage, the anxiety of waiting for her fantasy to begin would work her nerves.

She arrived after the luau had already been in full swing. She had lucked out and found an unoccupied table, slightly tucked away from the crowd yet close enough to enjoy the festively garbed hula group entertaining the crowd with Hawaiian folk music.

Gratefully, she sat at the table alone, neither seeking nor wanting any companionship. Despite the many invitations from the occasional earnest man who asked within moments of her sitting down.

She felt a prickling down her spine, and, with the uncanny ability that women had, felt an intent stare. She casually turned in her chair, her eyes scanning the crowd, and had discovered a set of intense gray eyes intently observing her. As Chase caught eyes with him, she hadn't been able to look away. For that brief moment a wave of electric awareness seem to arc between them.

More than a bit disturbed, she forced herself to look away and blindly gave her attention to the musicians on the stage. After their song ended, she was to turn around, only to discover the man gone. She dismissed the accompanying feeling of disappointment as soon as she felt it.

She only had that one moment to see him, yet she wouldn't forget his piercing stare, or the moment of connection between them.

"Is this seat taken?" he asked, looking down at her.

One side of his wide mouth hitched up in a smile as he indicated the throw she had spread over the sand as a makeshift beach blanket.

"No," she murmured, clearing her throat as she shifted her body to allow him room on the blanket. "Feel free."

She nonchalantly studied him as he hunkered down, situating his long body on the throw.

He was casually dressed in a simple white cotton shirt, the top buttons undone to reveal a sprinkling of silky dark hair on his broad, muscled chest, and a pair of snug dark jeans molding his hard thighs.

Chase moved her eyes over the large bulge between his legs that strained his zipper and the slightly more worn area around his crotch before allowing her eyes to reverse their trail up his body, just as he was turning toward her after sitting down.

He faced her, and twin, small creases slashed his lean cheeks—the small smile which hitched one side of his lips upward still in place.

Chase returned the slight smile before she turned away and wrapped her arms around her bent knees.

Gazing out at the cerulean blue water that sparkled like diamonds against the rays of the early morning sun, she said, "I've never seen anything so breathtaking. It's beautiful."

"It is," he agreed.

Chase turned slightly, only to discover that his eyes weren't on the water, but instead, watching her with that same intent concentration she'd felt at the luau. She stared at him, unable to move her eyes away. Tingling awareness shot down her body again. She shivered despite the warm, early morning sun beating down on her.

Forcing herself to look away from him, she turned back toward the water, and adjusted the fabric wrap more securely around her body.

"Is it everything you expected?"

Chase frowned, glancing at him from the corner of her eye. "What do you mean?"

"This—" He waved, sweeping a hand out, encompassing the beach, the water, the island.

"I don't know that I knew what to expect." The sigh escaped her before she could prevent it.

He released a low, deep chuckle, one that caused a rash of goosebumps to dance along her skin. She tightened her hold around her knees. "It is quite a different experience, isn't it? A very…unique experience."

Chase turned considering eyes on him. "What did *you* expect?" She wondered if he too were here for a fantasy getaway, and if so, what his fantasy was.

He was silent for so long that she doubted he'd answer. When he did, his answer was different than she'd expected.

"The same thing as you, I would imagine."

"And that would be?"

When he said nothing, she prodded further. "You're here for…" She allowed the question to dangle, not satisfied with his lack of a real answer.

"To have a fantasy fulfilled. A fantasy that if it does become fulfilled, it will not be for me alone."

"Oh? So you're a philanthropist?" She turned and faced him, raising a sardonic brow in question.

He laughed. "I wouldn't go that far. Let's just say that in fulfilling a fantasy of mine, it will also help fulfill the...unknown...fantasy of another."

"They don't know what they want?" Chase quickly picked up on his slight emphasis on fulfilling an *unknown* fantasy of another.

"On some level, perhaps."

Chastity pondered his statement. Before she could comment, he continued, "Do you always know what you want, Chastity?"

She bit her bottom lip, considering. "The same thing a lot of people want. I want to be on top. I've worked hard for everything I have achieved. I want recognition for it," she replied without thinking and immediately wondered what he thought of her bold statement.

He said nothing, but simply continued to stare out at the ocean. Although he didn't ask for any more information, Chase felt a need to explain.

"Is it so bad to want to be on the top? Is there anything wrong with wanting to be number one?"

"No, nothing wrong with that. But, before that happens, Chastity, you have to know yourself. You'll never get what you really want...what you deserve, if you don't free yourself of the demons of your past."

"What—what are you talking about?" Nearly speechless, Chase stammered the question.

He raised a long, lean finger and caressed a path down her face, his gaze locked with hers for long moments. Instead of flinching away, Chase found herself leaning into his touch. The moment she realized what she was doing, she brought herself up short and turned her head away, licking the bottom rim of her tongue in a state of confusion.

She heard him stand to leave and felt him staring down at her. She, however, forced herself not to look at him. After long moments, he turned and walked away.

Once she was sure he was gone, Chase turned her body to watch his retreating back as he walked toward the other end of the beach before disappearing behind the line of shrubbery, completely from her sight.

As she sat staring after him, it dawned on Chase that he'd called her by her first name. Her brows lowered and her forehead creased as she wondered how he knew her name.

A shiver of unknown awareness trickled down her spine.

CHAPTER 12

"We're here to bathe you."

Chastity's eyes snapped open with a start.

"Bathe me?" she muttered, licking her dry lips as she struggled to sit up.

She lifted her body from the sofa, where she'd fallen asleep after returning home from the beach. The warm sun and the mimosa she'd drunk had mingled to put her into such a relaxed state that she had dozed off to sleep within minutes of lying on the sofa.

Standing before her were two women wearing identical pleasant expressions on their beautiful faces and identical clothing of short, sheer, white gowns. But that was where the similarities ended.

One was tall, nearly as tall as Chase, and appeared to be of Asian heritage. Her dark, slanted eyes stared at Chase as she tightened the ties of her wrap around her body. Chase ran her eyes over the woman, from head to toe. She had porcelain-white, pale skin, yet beneath the sheer gown she wore, Chase could clearly see the imprint of her small, high breasts, tipped with small, cherry-wine-colored nipples that pressed against the sheer fabric.

Her eyes trailed down the woman's body, noting the small indenture of her waist and soft flaring of slender hips. At the juncture of her thighs, barely discernible, she saw a sprinkling of light-colored hair that covered her mound, which matched the color of her long, waist-length, rich, sable-colored hair.

Chase turned to the other woman, who silently appraised her as well. This one was petite and African American. The top of her closely cropped, curly hair barely reached her companion's shoulder.

Where her companion was boyishly slender, this one was the exact opposite. Her body was lushly curved beneath the sheer gown. Her waist was small and tightly nipped in with richly curved hips, and thick, toned legs. Chase's eyes rolled over her unbound breasts.

The large, perfectly rounded globes appeared firm, although they gently hung low, no doubt due to their massive size. Her chocolate-brown nipples, several shades darker than her creamy café au lait complexion, strained against the fabric.

A bloom of fiery lust unfurled deep in her belly as she surveyed the two beautiful attendants standing before her.

"My name is Aisha," the petite, brown beauty spoke in a low, husky voice. "This is LuAhn," she said, nodding her head toward the tall woman at her side, smiling a dazzling smile, exposing tiny, perfectly white teeth.

Chase swallowed the hazy desire threatening to overcome her as she surveyed the women before her. "What do you mean 'bathe me'?"

Neither woman replied. The one named LuAhn offered a hand, and Chase hesitantly placed hers within the woman's, allowing her to help her to rise.

Once she stood, both women bracketed her, one in front, the other in back, and quickly divested her of her clothing. Deft fingers moved over Chase's body with such cool efficiency that they had her completely nude before she could utter a protest.

"Come, let's go." The smaller one—Aisha—grasped her hand again and tugged, leading Chase toward the bedroom. Both women laid her on the bed and quickly joined her.

"I don't need you to bathe me. I—"

Soft hands pressed her down to the bed, and the women followed, lying on either side of her, front and back, sandwiching her. She felt the lushness of Aisha's body against her breasts, the soft curls covering her mound hotly pressed against Chase's own, and one muscular leg knifed Chase's thighs apart as her body molded and conformed to Chase's.

At the same time, the hard-body LuAhn pressed tightly against Chase's back, her mound contouring to Chase's buttocks, and her thighs nestled against the back of Chase's legs. One long, lean leg wrapped securely around one of Chase's calves.

"You will," the soft promise came from behind her.

A pair of pale hands firmly cupped Chase's breasts, tugging on her sensitive nipples, as a dark hand reached between her thighs, and numbly able fingers delved deep inside her core.

Chase moaned, and pressed closer to Aisha and her driving fingers. LuAhn lifted one of her breasts. Aisha's greedy mouth fastened on, making wet, kittenish sounds of delight as she feasted on Chase, her tongue lapping around the flat disk of her areole before tugging on Chase's tightening nipple.

After one final, sweet lick, the smaller woman released her hold on Chase's breast. Chase's body was slightly repositioned, so that she lay against LuAhn, while Aisha snaked her nimble body down the length of Chase's body until she reached the juncture of her legs.

Chase's eyes flew opened as the woman nipped her clit with the tips of her small teeth before using her tongue to soothe and stroke once, deeply into her cunt.

"Sssh, it's okay," LuAhn whispered hotly against Chase's ear as Chase began to fight against it, pushing away from LuAhn and leaning down to try and bring the dark beauty back toward her.

"No…stop." She breathed the words while trying again to pull the woman's bobbing head away from her, only to have LuAhn grab her hands and anchor them to her sides, forcing her to allow the other to continue.

"I…I…can't—" Chase bit the words out. "Not again."

"Give in to it," LuAhn encouraged.

Chase moved her head to look away, but LuAhn wouldn't allow her. She turned her face so that she had no choice but to watch.

Aisha placed both of her small hands beneath the globes of Chastity's buttocks, her eyes glued to Chase's, and with agonizing slowness leaned down toward the dark, curly thatch of hair at the apex of Chase's thighs.

Chase's nostrils flared, her heart slammed a staccato beat against her chest as she waited to feel her tongue against her pussy.

Her pointed tongue speared directly into Chase, her tongue hollowing as she scooped out a measure of her sweet cream.

A sigh of pleasure whispered past Chase's lips before she could prevent its escape.

She swallowed, her breath coming out in harsh gasps as she fought against the panic she felt begin to swamp her mind. It was too soon. She couldn't do this again…

Closing her eyes, she inhaled a deep, calming breath.

She then leaned back against LuAhn, forcing her body, her mind, to relax and gradually allowed her legs to relax as well, giving the woman and her devouring tongue silent acquiesce to continue.

"It's good?" LuAhn whispered the words, more of a statement than question, against Chase's neck. "You're enjoying this, yes?" Her tone was eager, as though her only wish, her only thought, was to please Chase.

Chase was silent, unable to say anything, warring emotions rendering her speechless. Aisha turned her head, looking to LuAhn for approval. She felt LuAhn nod her head, and like the eager pup she appeared to be, Aisha smiled happily and returned to feast between Chase's legs.

LuAhn's hands began to mold and massage Chase's breasts as Aisha devoured and lapped at her pussy in exquisite perfect orchestration.

LuAhn's firm but soft hands firmly massaged and played with her breasts, tugging and pulling on nipples that were taut and blood-filled, while Aisha's lips caressed her down below in slick, hot glides.

When the eager Aisha slipped a finger inside her ass, still going at her pussy with her velvet tongue, Chase gasped, pushing back into LuAhn's embrace.

LuAhn removed one hand from Chase's breasts and turned her face and slanted her mouth over Chase's, swallowing her whimpers of protests and pleasure.

The woman struck her tongue deep into Chase's mouth, and Chase eagerly latched on, their tongues dueling, chasing each other, as the kiss exploded.

"Yes, I think she is enjoying it," Chase heard the dark woman between her thighs murmur in response to the question she'd asked. She felt the woman's smile against her thighs, but no longer cared. She simply wanted her to keep doing what she was doing.

Chase reached a hand down and planted it at the top of the dark woman's head, not to draw away from her, as she'd done in the past; instead to draw her nearer, shamelessly grinding her vagina against the woman's face.

She bucked and ground her lower body while exchanging hot, torrid kisses with the beautiful Asian woman, the pleasure humming through her body was so strong, so…intense, tears burned the back of her eyes.

When Aisha lifted her thighs higher, placing them over her shoulder, and fucked her in tight licks, adding a second finger to dig further into her clenching ass, Chase clenched her eyes shut. Yet she continued to allow the women to work her, fuck her, fully participating in the threesome as the women catered to her, doing her so good, a cry of pleasure ripped from her throat.

With determined licks and prods of her tongue, the woman between her thighs continued to eat and suck, devouring her pussy in earnest. Humming softly buzzed in Chase's ears as her body began to tremble, the beginnings of an orgasm unfurling.

She swallowed, her muscles tensing; the legs she had around Aisha clamped down on either side of her face.

Panicking, Chase grunted in protest against the woman's mouth when she tried to escape the passionate clutches of both women.

She broke the kiss, and frantically shoved against the woman between her thighs, pulling at her head, desperately trying to escape the impeding orgasm.

But neither woman allowed her to escape.

The one holding her captive grasped her arms and pulled them behind her head. With smooth dexterity, she grabbed the gown she'd discarded near the floor and knotted Chase's hands together, effectively securing them above her head.

In desperation, realizing what was happening, Chase fought against the makeshift restraints to no avail.

LuAhn slammed her mouth over Chase's, roughly grasped her blood-tightened nipples between her fingers and pulled. The painful tug caused electric pulses to radiate through her body. At the same time, Aisha pulled her clit deep into her mouth and lightly bit the engorged nub before releasing it. She peeled back the lips of her vagina, laving her inner lips, and immediately began to feed Chase her fingers, one at a time until she'd imbedded them all, stuffing her small, balled fist deep into Chase's cunt.

The woman returned to a slow screwing, her balled fists dragging in and out of Chase's core as her mouth gave short, almost delicate swipes to her outer vaginal lips.

The orgasm hit, without warning, slamming her back against the woman who cradled her in her arms.

She screamed into LuAhn's mouth as she ground herself, impaled herself on Aisha's fist, grinding against her; her body bucked and spasmed as the release washed over her.

Once her body completed, drowsy, she lay back, exhausted against LuAhn's body, her chest moving in and out in deep breaths at the lazily swirling overhead fan.

She didn't protest as they lifted her as though her weight was nothing and carried her into the bathroom.

After filling the large, Jacuzzi-styled tub, the three women, as though in a rehearsed erotic play, climbed into the tub.

The women immediately began to wash her. Aisha began to clean her feet, as she lay against LuAhn, both of their soft hands feathering over her body in caresses so light they felt like butterflies whispering over Chase's skin.

She closed her eyes and allowed them to cater to her. When she felt the soapy towel between her thighs, nudging against them, she opened her legs, willingly, knowing what the women wanted.

She moaned when she felt the sponge slip between the swollen lips of her vagina, yet didn't stop her.

LuAhn ran a twin sponge down her breasts, and with a detached awareness, Chase watched the soapy trail of suds trickle between the valley of her breasts, down the mid line of her body, before disappearing in the water near her hips.

"I think you're ready for him," LuAhn whispered against her ear.

Chase's eyes snapped opened, the relaxing nearly euphoric feeling evaporating at the woman's words.

CHAPTER 13

With methodical precision, Chase folded her clothes neatly, placing them in her opened suitcase. After she'd finished, she placed her toiletry bag on top, and with a definitive snap, she closed her suitcase, snapping the lock into place.

She glanced around the room, making sure she hadn't forgotten anything, before lifting the case from the bed, placing it on the bedroom floor.

She exhaled a long breath.

She had to get out.

Enough was damn enough.

After the women had left, LuAhn's words rang into her head, long into the day, and the following night. *"I think you're ready for him..."*

She'd been on edge, waiting and wondering what was to come next. In the end, she decided that she no longer wanted to play puppet in someone's twisted game.

"This is *my* fantasy. I didn't come here to be a pawn or made to submit to someone else's agenda," she murmured out loud.

She picked up the phone and not knowing what else to do, merely going on blind instinct, punched the number for the operator. Immediately she was connected with a woman who identified her by name, and solicitously asked how she could serve her.

"You can *serve* me by getting me the hell out of this place. Now."

There was a long pause before the woman replied in a cheerful voice, "I'm sorry, Ms. Davidson, but your fantasy has not reached its natural conclusion. You—"

"Natural conclusion, my ass. Bitch, if you do *not* get me off this island, *now*..." Chase clamped her mouth shut and took in deep breaths, futilely attempting to bring her temper under control.

There was deafening silence, then a series of clicks...

"Is there a problem, Ms. Davidson?" the smooth deep voice of the man she knew to be Merrick asked.

"Yes. You could say that!" Chase proceeded to outline, in precise detail, what the problem was, concluding with, "I didn't sign up for this, Merrick. I didn't sign up to be gang-raped and forced to do shit—"

"You were gang-raped? Forced to do things against your will, Ms. Davidson?" he smoothly interjected, his voice calm, neutral.

Chase shut her eyes and gritted her teeth.

Chase sighed. She sat down on the bed, shoving the suitcase to the side.

She refused to give him the satisfaction by admitting she had become an all-too-willing participant in the sexual games. "This isn't what I thought it would be. Nothing has been as I thought it would be."

"Did you not ask to be number one? Wasn't that your desire, to be in demand, every need catered to...to be number one?" he asked, his voice silky and smooth.

"Not like this! I—"

"Do you *not* remember what your invitation stated, Ms. Davidson?"

Chase opened her mouth to tell him exactly what she thought of the *invitation*, but before she could, he continued to speak.

"Should you choose to accept this invitation, you agree that you are succumbing to your desires, that you are freeing yourself to experience something you've never dared to yield to," he reminded her of the last clause in the invitational contract.

"So does that mean I'm forced to stay here? Is *that* what the hell you're telling me?" she spat in agitation.

"Ms. Davidson, at the conclusion of your fantasy, your charter plane will arrive to safely escort you off the island."

Seconds later, a buzzing tone hummed in her ear, indicating he'd disconnected the line, leaving a bemused Chase on the other end.

She'd pressed the dial button ready to call him back, to let him know just what she thought of his island. This was supposed to be a fantasy where she was number one, where she called the shots.

"Damn it!" she snarled.

She hurled the phone against the wall and in satisfaction watched it break into a hundred shattered pieces and fall to the floor.

CHAPTER 14

"I don't think I've ever seen water so blue."

Chase experienced a thrill when she heard the deep voice from behind her. She hadn't heard his approach, yet she wasn't surprised that he was there.

She turned, glancing over her shoulder, and made eye contact with the man who stood near.

Not only was his appearance anticipated, Chase had hoped she would see him. In her subconscious she knew she would come to the beach again, at the same time in the hope of seeing him again.

She didn't want to leave the island without seeing him one final time. And she had every intent on leaving the island today, even if that meant she had to swim across to the main island.

"No, I can't say that I have. But then again, everything about this island is…*different*."

"Magical?"

"Hmmm," she hummed the non-committal response.

"May I?"

He didn't wait for a reply, but simply folded his large frame down to sit closely beside her.

"Different in what way?"

She turned, her features twisting, eyebrows scrunched as she considered his response. After he'd settled, she turned away, staring at the sun as it settled behind the calm, dark, azure waters.

"Maybe surreal is a more apt way to describe it," she replied and shrugged. "Damned if I know." She laughed without any real humor.

They sat in companionable silence for long moments as they gazed at the gentle waves slapping against one another in the otherwise calm ocean waters.

"Have you ever worked so hard for something only to have it snatched away from you, along with all of your dreams crashing down around you?" Chase asked, shivering when the wind rose and wrapping her arms more snuggly around her bent knees.

She felt him shift on the blanket and draw nearer. When one strong arm wrapped around her shoulders, it felt good to lean against him, to soak in his warmth. It seemed natural to allow him the intimacy. To allow the intimacy of a stranger.

"I have." His answer, although short, increased the feeling of *rightness* she'd felt around him, from the moment they'd met. As though they were kindred spirits, of sorts. She shrugged off the uncomfortable thought and shifted her body so that his arm fell away. He made no response, yet she felt his gaze.

"Well, welcome to my world." She laughed, without humor, turning back to look at him. "I guess that's why I jumped at the chance to come here. Nothing like mindless sex to take your mind off your problems," she finished flippantly.

His eyes intently roamed over her face as though seeking the answer to some unknown question. Chase shivered beneath his intent stare.

"No. That's not why you came. There had to be more to it than mindless sex."

Chase exhaled a long breath. Closing her eyes, her hands flattened on the blanket as she leaned back in thought. "No. That's not why I came."

He said nothing, and the silence, the semi-deserted beach, and his strangely comforting presence aided in creating an atmosphere that compelled Chase to speak out loud about the things that were on her mind—easily.

"I lost something that I'd been working all my life for." She released a humorless laugh. "I suppose it was something I was able to measure myself against, to measure my success against. When I didn't get it, a lot of things changed for me, things I'm still trying to understand and get a grasp on it. Hell, I'm still not sure what or why it all happened." She began to tell him of the events that had transpired over the last week of her life, events that had turned her world upside down.

"It's in those moments that you have to take a hard look at your life. You know, when your world comes crashing in. When you—" She stopped.

Self-conscious, realizing that she'd just told a complete stranger things she'd never discussed with anyone, things she'd kept hidden away from herself.

The thought was disconcerting. "God, I'm sorry. Didn't mean to deliver a diatribe."

"No need to apologize. I suppose that's a good enough reason as any to re-evaluate your life," he replied smoothly, the genuine warmth in his voice reassuring.

She continued to speak, finding it easy to talk to him, to unload things she'd kept buried deep inside for years. She told him things she'd never spoken out loud, things she never documented in a personal journey. Things she normally tried to avoid all thoughts of.

In doing so, she felt a portion of her curious burden lift from her shoulders.

"You grew up alone." Chase turned to look at him. He offered the question more like a statement.

"It was just me and my mother for a long time. When I was a bit older, my mother remarried. My father didn't re-enter the picture until I was older," she answered, swallowing against the bile that rose to her throat immediately. She ruthlessly suppressed the revulsion…the fear.

"Did things change when he came back into your life?"

Chase laughed, harshly, no longer seeing the handsome, enigmatic man beside her. Instead she saw the mocking image of the one who was supposed to protect her, the one who'd been the one who had hurt her, had been instrumental in damaging her in ways that went far beyond the physical.

"Yes," she answered softly, painful memories of just how well she'd gotten to know her father piercing her heart.

She ground her teeth together, batting her eyelashes and frantically forcing to prevent the tears she felt threatening to break through, to remain tightly leashed.

"Look, I need to go," she said, feeling a desperate need to get away from him and his intent stare.

She hastily got to her feet and quickly retrieved her things after he moved away from the blanket. Silently, he watched her as she dumped the blanket inside the tote bag she'd carried to the beach.

"Thanks for the free therapy," she said glibly and ignored

the look he gave her. "But, I think it's time for me to go." She said the words with finality. It was not only time for her to get away from him and her strange attraction to him, but to get as far away from the island as she could get.

She turned to leave, not waiting—not wanting—to hear his reply. She'd only taken a few steps away when his words stopped her.

"Success comes with a price, Chastity. What price are you willing to pay?"

Chase faltered in her steps at his words, and stopped. She turned her head, so that she could see him in her peripheral vision.

"I'm willing to pay whatever price is necessary."

CHAPTER 15

Chase sat in one of the swivel-backed chairs of the kitchen's small dinette table, staring out of one of the windows, overlooking the beach.

"What price am I willing to pay to succeed?" she said out loud in a low voice, recalling his words.

She didn't need a trip to her therapist to know that her need to be in control had long been an obsession and was what drove her every action, her every step. The obsession had invaded not only her professional life. Her unquenchable desire and thirst to be successful had also shaped her personal life, twisting her in ways she hadn't realized.

It went beyond the sexual. Chase knew that the root of her problem was embedded in her childhood, yet it had been something she'd refused to acknowledge, much less try and get resolution for.

She'd allowed her past to shape her present—to the point that her world was now tumbling down around her.

Before the events of the last few days, Chase had been confident of who she was, had been so confident that there wasn't a man...or woman...who could control or manipulate her.

First, there'd been Javier. She had been certain he was well controlled, that she was the one in charge…*Overly so, obviously*, she thought and laughed harshly. She picked up the coffee and took a careful sip of the steaming brew before thoughtfully placing it back down on the glass table.

She'd been confident that he was faithful to her, assured that she could trust him. That she'd *trained* him well. She had molded him, carefully manipulated the relationship, ensuring his dependence on her, dominating him to ensure his dependence on her. And in the end…

"In the damn end, he screwed me. Just like he said." She laughed without humor.

She pushed herself away from the table and stood. *God, what was she going to do?*

Padding barefoot over to the small sink, she placed the mug inside and turned on the tap, rinsing out the cup and stopped herself.

Even now, she had to have everything neat, in order. Everything in her world always had to neat, exact, orderly.

After leaving the beach, her conversation with—*God, she didn't even know the man's name*, she thought—ran through her mind.

She had no idea what would await her when she accepted the invitation to come to Ka-le'a. Her only thought had been to get away from the devastation that had become her life, in a matter of hours. The very enticing thought of being number one, even sexually, had swayed her, at a time when she needed a quick ego stroke.

Instead, she'd been forced to deal with her own demons, had been forced to submit and allow others to pleasure her. In doing so she'd been forced to release and give up her own power, the power she'd worked her entire life to maintain. And she found pleasure in doing so. As much as she hated to think about it, much less acknowledge it, she found it strangely exhilarating. But, the thought of her "final" adventure, the one that the others hinted at, was unsettling.

She straightened her back. She'd come this far in her journey; there was no way in hell she was going to back out now.

With a sigh, she turned away and as she walked toward the living area, she turned when she heard the back door of the patio open.

Her eyes widened, and her heart slammed against her chest when she saw the man lounging against the doorway, his light-gray eyes staring at her. No emotion crossed his handsome face.

"You. I should have known."

CHAPTER 16

She stood there, immobile, staring at the lounging form of the man in the doorway whose gray-eyed gaze seared a burning, betraying hole that painfully pierced her heart.

Thinking back, it all made sense. Of course it was him. Who else would it be?

"So what—who—are you?" she asked, staring at the man who was a stranger, yet not.

Her question was met with a silence that angered her even more.

"Why me?" The words were torn from behind tightly clenched teeth.

She turned away, unable to look at him. She felt vulnerable… naked, despite that she was fully clothed. Her stomach churned and her head throbbed with a sudden ache as she thought of how she'd exposed herself to him. The way she'd told him some of her deepest thoughts. Thoughts she'd never shared with another living soul.

She'd poured out her heart thinking he was a complete stranger, finding it easy to reveal herself to him, in that way that came easier with strangers, falsely believing she would have no more interaction with him.

And all along he'd *known* who she was. "God damn you."

He had been the one to "buy" her. Her lips curled in a snarl as she spun around to face him, only to find him standing directly behind her. He'd moved silently, further into the room and now stood mere inches away from her. His hands settled on top of her shoulders. Flinching, she tore away from him.

"Don't fucking touch me," she spit the words and turned on her heels to move away. She'd only taken two steps away when his voice stopped her.

"Don't go. Please."

The simple command prevented her from moving.

"And if I do?" she asked, without turning back around.

Silence met her question. She waited, wondering to what lengths he'd go to keep her.

"You can't go, Chase. To do so would be admitting defeat. You're too strong of a woman for that."

"What do you know about me or my strengths?" She hurled the words at him turning to face him. "You don't know shit about me!" She reached out and slapped him as hard as she could, her hand leaving a burning red imprint on his lean cheek.

He swallowed. His jaw tightened so that the muscle twitched. But, he said nothing. That angered Chase even more.

"What? You're just going to take it? Nothing to say?" She pushed him, her anger escalating.

She shoved her flattened hands against the steel wall of his chest, as angry tears ran down her face in rivulets. Balling her fists, in earnest she fought him, until she stumbled and fell to the floor, bringing him down with her.

He swiftly maneuvered their bodies, ripping the fabric wrap dress she wore so that her breasts came tumbling free. He trapped her beneath him.

"Enough!" he bit out, grabbing her hands and securing them above her head; his hard chest blanketing her now naked body.

Her chest heaved as she took in deep breaths. The wood floor was cold against her naked breasts, and his hard back was warm against her back, yet she wasn't going to allow him to dominate her. She'd had enough of that.

Chase waited for long moments, enough to catch her breath, before she renewed her struggles. Surprising him, she slammed her head back, catching the side of his face and snatched her hands away from his grip.

She bucked against him, throwing him off her body, enough so that she was able to get on her hands and knees and crawl away from him.

"Come back here," he growled, grabbing her legs, pulling her roughly back toward him as she crawled along the floor.

Chase didn't waste energy speaking.

She kicked one leg behind her, blindly, and heard the satisfying sound of connecting with some part of his body. He grunted, but kept coming after her.

She rose and made a mad dash toward the patio door. Seconds away from opening the door, she felt him grasp her around the waist. He spun her around, his hold unyielding as he dragged her back against him. Crushing her body to his, he slammed their joined bodies against the wall.

"That's the last time you get away with that." The hard, determined look on his angry face sent thrills of fear and anticipation racing over Chase's body.

His hands roamed over her, familiarizing himself with the lush lines of her curves, running his hands over her back, over the nipped-in indenture of her waist, and over the smooth, muscled contours of her ass.

He grabbed the ties of her dress and tore them, pulling the dress from her body.

"You won't need these, either," he said before ripping her thong off her body, staring into her eyes, his expression intense.

She gasped when he pressed against her, and slipped one thick finger past her creaming folds, plunged deep inside her pussy, and scooped a measure of her cum out, flickering her blood-thickened clit, spreading the dewy moisture around it.

He trailed his finger down her perineum, the sensitive skin between her pussy and ass, and Chase bit back a moan of pleasure when he rimmed her tight, puckered hole, feathering against it, teasing her.

Before she could utter a protest, he had her back down on the floor, she in front of him, on her hands and knees with him behind her.

She heard the hiss of his zipper and glanced over her shoulder to see him impatiently pull his slacks down the length of his legs, far enough so that his angry cock jutted free. His hands quickly went to his shirt, pulling it over his head and exposing his broad, thick, muscled chest before he brought her body back into tight alignment with his.

She swallowed, deeply, when the impressive, hard length of his dick probed impatiently at her pussy, demanding entrance.

He grabbed her hair, fisted the long strands like a rope around his hand and pulled her head back, so that she was forced to look at him. Her heart thudded erratically against her chest, as she took in his tightly drawn features, the look of lust and determination gleaming sharply in his eyes in the dark room. He placed a scorching kiss on the side of her neck, and Chase moaned, her eyes fluttering closed.

He ran his tongue down her neck and the column of her throat before retracing his path. He swirled a delicious, hot pattern inside her ear, taking the fleshy lobe into his mouth, and biting sharply. The sting was negligible, but it was enough for her to feel it. Cream ran down the inside of her thighs.

"You're not angry with me. You're angry with yourself," he whispered the words against the sensitive hollow beneath her ear.

He pushed her back down and clamped a hand over the back of her neck, stilling her. "You're angry because what you *thought* you wanted, you didn't get."

The ends of Chase's nostrils flared; her breathing hitched as she listened to him speak. The words shot a piercing arrow directly to her heart.

"You're angry because you knew that all along."

He began to feed her his dick in painstakingly slow, scorching inches, until he filled her, stuffing her, until she felt every hard inch and he bumped the back of her womb. She shut her eyes tightly; her hands and arms shook as she accepted him deep into her body.

"You had to be broken down. You had to be *forced* to reevaluate who you are. Why you are."

The more he spoke, as his strokes intensified in strength and power, the more her body began to ripple, blossom.

"Only then would you be ready. Only then can you be the true woman you were destined to be."

Chase pushed back against his dick, seeking to devour him as much as he was devouring her with his cock and his words. The scent of sex and lust made her dizzy. Stars began to unfold behind the tightly clenched lids of her eyes.

He pushed her down on the floor and ground into her, riding her ass, fucking her fiercely, her clit rubbing against the wood floor as he rode her. At the angle he had her, with her ass slightly raised off the floor, pressed out so he could fuck her, her pussy and clit mashed against the cold floor, as he ground into her.

"Yes...yes," she cried out against his thrusts as her pussy milked his dick.

"You're so ripe, so juicy," he bit the words out as he pumped into her in long strokes. She heard his breathing, as harsh and loud as her own, as he steadily drove into her.

He jammed her body, driving into her seeping hole until his balls tapped her ass, unrelenting in his dominance over her, surging into her welcoming heat.

"So wet, but so tight," he bit the words out.

His hard hand roughly smoothed over her ass before he separated the round, high cheeks of her ass, running a finger down until he reached her seeping vagina

"Oh, God...yes, yes..." she moaned as he moved in and out of her in easy, sure glides.

Her body jostled and her knees scraped against the hardwood floors as his strokes became hotter, harder, more demanding. Had he not held on to her, her body would have completely lifted off the floor with the strength of his strokes. Chase pushed back against him, her cunt gripping and milking his rigid cock as he knifed into her with powerful able slices.

Her thighs quivered, her breath came out in strangled gasps, her nostrils flared as the scent of sex and his unique smell covered her. Overwhelmed her.

She moaned and cried out against the power of his thrusts, raising herself onto her elbows as she bucked back against him, loving every minute of the glorious fucking.

His thrusts were so powerful, so harsh, they bordered on painful, yet she shoved back into him, rolled her hips against his marauding cock to capture every thriving thrust. Her breasts swayed, jostling, the tips of her nipples brushing on the floor with each shove of his dick inside.

"Yes, yes...harder....just like that," she gasped, and shouted when she felt the stinging slap of a hard hand against one of her butt cheeks. Her keening cries rang loudly in the room when he delivered another stinging slap to her bottom. She screamed, the pleasure intensifying to incredulous portions, her body on fire, sweat dripping down her face.

As he fucked her, he continued to slap her ass, harder, in rhythm to his corkscrew thrusts until the pain and pleasure mingled into one, sending her body over the edge, shattering her. Crystal-like stars flashed in front of her, her mind and body shattering into a million shards of glass as the power of her release shook her.

Behind her, he continued to dig into her, lifting one of her legs to reposition her as he angled his marauding cock at a new angle. He pumped into her—hard, fast, mercilessly. Chase felt another orgasm rip, tearing into her. She screamed as he held on to her tightly.

As she came a second time, she heard his hoarse shout from behind her and seconds later his cum, hot, scorching, sweet, landed in hot streams on her back.

Chase lay on her stomach, with his body pressing her into the floor, limp and utterly satiated. She shivered as their combined sweat began to cool, shivering in reaction to the wild sex and the man who had thoroughly and completed dominated her.

Later, they lay on the bed, sweaty and exhausted. One of his hard legs was horizontally across hers, pinning her to the bed while an arm rested over her waist. His penis, now softened, lay against her buttocks.

He'd taken her again, on the floor, soon after the first episode. The second time he'd fucked her, his erection had been as rigid, just as unyielding as the first time, as though the sexing he'd given her moments earlier hadn't happened.

It had been quick, hot and hard, as he'd rutted her like a dog. And like a bitch in heat, she'd welcomed him into her body until she'd exploded, taking him with her.

It had been much later that she'd felt him lift her satiated body from the floor and carry her into the bedroom, carefully laying her on the bed, before he'd lain behind her, bringing her body flush against his as they'd drifted to sleep.

Now, as she awoke, and she was no longer caught in the sensual, fiery web of lust and sex, the shame of her complete submission stung.

He moved up her body, snaked his way up her body, and nudged between her legs, pushing them up until her feet were planted on the bed, with her knees bent and raised.

He saw that she was watching, and kept his eyes on hers as he bent his head toward her mound. She inhaled a deep breath, her lips partially opened, her heart thudding, as she waited to feel his mouth on that part of her body that longed for his touch.

"Hmmm," she moaned, arching her back, when he tongued aside the swollen lips of her vagina, the flat of his tongue swiping against her moist folds.

Kneeling between her bent knees, he ran a callused finger

up her inner thigh in soft strokes, until he reached the wiry, closely cut hairs that surrounded her vagina. He drew the finger up the seam of her pussy, gently splitting her open to his watchful gaze. He brought his other hand up, to keep her pussy open, and with the other stroked her distended nub.

Her body responded instantly. Her breath came out in harsh sighs. She felt her face flush in arousal and within seconds, she felt the ease of cream as it dripped from her pussy, and ran down his hand. He lifted his head, one side of his long, sensual mouth hitched. Keeping his eyes trained on hers, he licked his finger of her dewy essence.

"Sweet...bold, enticing. Just like you," he murmured, before turning his gaze back between her thighs.

He fingered her clit, toying and pinching the erect nub until Chase wanted to scream, beg him to take it into his mouth, beg him to bring her to release. But, she stopped herself.

Although every cell in her body, every nerve ending was on fire, begging for him to take her, she clenched her teeth and stopped herself from begging him.

The tormenting pleasure was one she *wanted* to endure.

She wanted him to string her out, wanted him to force her to accept his petting, his teasing. She knew that when he finally gave her what she wanted...*needed*...the release would be that much more pleasurable.

His tongue snaked out and licked her, from the back of her pussy to the front, in one long, hot stroke that had her back peeling off the bed, a cry on her lips.

He leaned back in, and blew a warm breath across her mound, tickling the wiry hairs, and more of her cream eased, running down her thighs. Sounds of pleasure came from his throat as his tongue darted out and quickly lapped her cream.

She clenched her legs in response, only to have him widen them, forcing her knees to spread wide, giving him more room.

This time he used his fingers to separate her, opening the lips of her vagina as he lapped at her streaming core in slick strokes.

Chase leaned back and accepted his oral loving, her hands balled on either side of her body as she fisted the silk sheets in each hand.

He suckled her clit deep into his mouth, his teeth scraping and pulling at the engorged little bud, and then inserted a finger deep inside. Chase bucked against his face, released her hold on the sheets, and grabbed both sides of his face, grinding against him as he continued to lave, suckle, and stroke her.

When the pressure built until she thought she couldn't handle it anymore, he inserted two more fingers deep into her channel; another until he was knuckle deep inside, dragging his curled fingers in and out of her until she broke.

The orgasm slammed into her.

"Yes. Yes!" she screamed, her upper body coming off the bed as she grabbed his head, grinding and pumping her hips against him, as the orgasm slammed into her. He pinched her clit, completely slamming her over the edge, yet continued to eat her pussy.

Even as the tremors began to ease, he lapped at her until she lay spent on the bed.

He delivered one final, hot lick into her core and her body completed its release. He climbed on top of her, leaned down and kissed her, gently on the mouth.

She felt her own essence as he gently kissed her on the mouth.

"Was it worth it?" Chase asked, as she lay next to him.

He looked down at her, raising a dark-brown brow in question.

"Twenty-five million is a lot to pay for a lay."

"Is that all you think this was about?" he asked.

"I don't know anything. You seem to know a lot about me, but I don't know anything about you. Why all of this? Why pay that much money for me?"

"Don't you think you're worth it?"

"Please don't do that."

"What?"

"Turn it around on me. I asked you an upfront question. Or is this something you do often? Pay for sex..."

"No." He laughed lightly. "I've never paid for sex. I didn't pay for sex this time, either." His non-answer thoroughly confused her.

"Do you work for Merrick then? Was all of the bidding, the high bidding, all a part of the fantasy?" she asked, strangely hurt. She remembered how exhilarating it had felt when the price, the "bid," had escalated to millions; recalled the feeling to have a room full of people all desperate for her and her alone.

The thought that it had all been a pretense, that the audience was all actors or whatever...

"It was real, Chase. All of it. The audience, the money, the bidding. All of it was very real, let me assure you."

His answer satisfied her.

"You must think I'm crazy. Wanting to be bought like a piece of merchandise," she said after a long silence, where she lay subdued beneath him, one of his hard legs thrown across her.

He reached down and lifted her chin so that she met his eyes. "No. I don't. Not at all."

Leaning down, he placed a soft kiss on her mouth, and Chase shut her eyes, accepting his kiss. When he broke the kiss, she leaned back down laying her head on his chest.

"You have nothing to be ashamed of. It was a fantasy that many shared with you. There is nothing wrong with you."

She remained quiet and allowed his reassuring words to soak in.

"Do you want me, Chastity?" he asked, his liquid brown eyes locked with hers.

Chase stared at him, uncertain. There was so much more to his question than appeared.

He was waiting for her to acknowledge that she was willing—that she wanted him to pleasure her, yes, but also that she was willing to allow him to break through that final barrier, one she'd kept so firmly in place, one she'd spent years erecting, one that guarded her from ever feeling at the mercy of another.

God, was she ready for that? Was she ready to let go, to allow another control over her body, her mind, her spirit?

Turmoil and anxiety were nothing new to her, particularly over the last few days as she'd been challenged to face the demons of her past.

She swallowed, her eyes roaming over his, before she succumbed.

Unable to speak, she simply nodded her head, in acquiesce.

With her acceptance, peace, serenity, overcame her. She wrapped her leg around his calf, slowly running her foot up his leg, to wrap around over his hard-muscled buttocks, and over his waist.

"Tell me," he demanded, "say it."

She looked in his eyes, desperately, clutching his broad shoulders. "Please..."

"Please what, Chastity?" He was unrelenting in his demands for her full submission.

She closed her eyes against what he was asking of her, what he was demanding for her to say.

He slanted his mouth over hers, swallowing her cry of distress as his tongue shoved past her teeth swiping into her mouth.

"I—I can't," she cried out, breaking away from his mouth.

He brought his hands up to frame her face, forcing her to look at him.

"Tell me, Chastity."

Chase swallowed down the need to rebel, to push him away. To deny him the ultimate access to her. "What makes you think you have a right to demand anything from me?"

"Tell me," he repeated the command, his tone firm, brooking no argument.

She bit her lip and stared at him. Instead of shoving away, she deliberately brought her leg up, running it slowly along his calf, the heel of her foot scraping along his calf, his thighs, before she wrapped her leg around his lean waist pulling their bodies closer.

"I want you to make me come," she whispered, looking directly into his eyes.

The smile he gave her was one of savage satisfaction.

Keeping eye contact with her, he grasped her hands in his, threading his fingers with hers and began to penetrate her.

He eased inside, gently and carefully as though she was fragile, delicate. As though she was cherished.

The sex was different this time. As he stroked into her, he maintained eye contact, taking her hands in his and threading their fingers together. He wouldn't allow her to look away as his hips rolled in slow, leisurely thrusts. He leaned down and kissed her, sliding his tongue as deeply into her mouth as his shaft was inside her body. He broke the kiss, his breath coming out in shallow pants that mimicked hers.

Carefully, he ground into her, setting a smooth, in-and-out rhythm that was nearly unbearable in its pleasure.

"Oh God, that feels so good." Chase panted the words, her hips matching his, thrust for thrust, as their bodies strained against each other. He reached down to pull one of her breasts deeply into his mouth, and Chase cried out sharply.

Between the hot feel of him shafting her and his tight pulls on her breasts, she didn't know how much longer she could take it. When he reached a hand between them and tugged on her clit, she broke.

She screamed as her orgasm slammed into her, her body jerking as the release took over. As she came, he continued to thrust into her until he too released. Hot streams of his cum washed her womb, as she lay beneath him satisfied and replete. Complete at last.

When she'd woken in the morning, she turned over in the bed, seeking him. Instead of his warm, large body cradling hers, she was alone.

She had a thousand questions to ask him. Who was he? Why had he come to the island? Why had he chosen her?

But none of those answers would she ever know.

She closed her eyes, hugged the pillow that held his unique scent to her body for long moments, and cried.

She didn't cry because he wasn't there. The tears were for

what he'd helped her to release. What he'd helped her achieve had been magical, something unreal, something she'd never forget.

Just as she'd never forget him.

"Ms. Davidson, we hope your stay here with us was pleasurable."

Chastity removed her sunglasses and smiled genuinely at Merrick.

She leaned her head down to allow the woman who stood at his side to present her with the traditional lei.

She laughed lightly, thinking of when she'd arrived, how she'd impatiently waved the woman away as she'd tried to "lei" her.

She grasped the hand he held out, holding onto it as she looked into his eyes. He smiled, his dark-brown eyes held the same hint of mystery she'd seen when she'd met him, yet to her frustration, she had been unable to decipher. Now, she knew. She mentally amended that. She had a small idea as it pertained to her. His job had been to help her free herself from the bonds—invisible bonds that had kept her restrained for so long, bonds that had limited her from fully coming into her own as a woman.

The rest was now up to her.

"Yes, it was indeed," she replied.

He simply nodded his head to her. Moments later, she turned with him, along with the others who stood waiting as the outer doors of the charter plane transporting them to Honolulu opened, ready to take them back.

She turned and ran her eyes over the small group, searching for *him*. Deep inside, she knew she wouldn't see him in the small crowd.

She batted away the tears that threatened to fall again and met Merrick's enigmatic stare. She doggedly forced a smile on her face.

When the attendant came to her side, she gave him her luggage, and with a final glance over the milling crowd, she turned and strode toward the plane.

CHAPTER 17

Chastity sat with her hands clenching the leathered wheel of her Mercedes, her eyes darting over the rundown, two-story, brick townhouse she called home for the first sixteen years of her life.

She released the death-grip she had on the wheel, cut off the softly humming engine, and pocketed her keys in her purse. And sat. Running her eyes back over the house, she knew her mother was home because her car sat in the driveway.

"God, what in hell am I doing here?" she spoke out loud, running a shaky hand over her loose hair, tucking a curl behind her ear.

What she hoped to accomplish, she didn't know.

She leaned back against the seat, thinking of her return from the island.

When she finally got home, her first order of business was to shower and fall into bed. As she went to retrieve one of the Hawaiian outfits she had purchased, an envelope fell out of the bag. She turned it over, and there was the invitation, the same one she'd gotten in email.

With her heart caught in her throat, she ran her fingers gently over the red wax seal with the blossoming hibiscus embossed in the center. She brought the sealed envelope to her nose, and her eyes feathered closed as the fragrant, distinct scent of the flower wafted into her nostrils.

With trembling hands, she split the seal, and pulled out the note. As she withdrew it, a lone hibiscus petal floated to the floor.

"And the day came when the risk to remain tight in a bud was more painful than the risk it took to blossom."

After reading the quote, the bitter tears she'd kept trapped for years fell freely.

She sat on the expensive ceramic tile in the middle of her living room and cried.

She cried tears of anger, humiliation, fear, and regret. The tears made her body jerk in spasms and her back bow in pain. Her plummeting fist pounded against the tile as the tears wracked her body.

She cried for the years she'd endured under her mother's care. She cried for the lost years of her youth. She cried for the little girl who had been forced to grow up before her time. She cried for the little girl who never had a mother and was victimized. She cried for the little girl who became an abuser and sought to be number one at all costs without realizing that she'd become no better than her mother. She cried as she realized that what she'd been seeking no one could give her. Peace.

Knowing that she'd never allow another to make her feel as though she was nothing, less than, she'd ruthlessly sought to be the one in control, the one to call the shots and to hell with any and everything else.

She'd cried for the little girl who'd grown up to believe that she was no good.

In her quest for control, she'd become lost, adrift...

She'd cried until her throat, her body, her mind and soul screamed out in painful protest.

She'd cried until she'd had no more tears left to cry.

After the tears had dried, she knew what she had to do. Something that was long overdue.

Now, with her hand on the handle of the door, she hesitated, glancing at the dilapidated house.

Taking a deep breath, she opened the door and briskly walked the short distance to the front door. That old familiar fear pooled and tied her gut in knots, yet she forced one foot in front of the other. Forced herself not to turn away and run back in her car and get the hell out of there.

She knocked on the door, and as fear tied her gut in knots, she waited.

CHAPTER 18

"What do you want? I ain't got no money so I can't buy nothin' you selling, so you may as well go on somewhere," the old woman mumbled, her thick fingers wrapped around the edge of the door. She held it opened just far enough for her to peer out.

"It's me." Chastity cleared her throat and spoke louder. "It's Chastity. Can I come in?"

"Chastity?" the woman asked, her watery eyes squinting as though she didn't recognize her.

"Yeah, it's me. Chase."

"Well, I was in the middle of cooking…" Maybelle's mumbles trailed away as she clutched together the ends of her frayed robe.

She spoke as though she didn't know Chase, as though she was being inconvenienced by Chase. As though she was a stranger and not her own daughter.

"I just wanted to talk to you for a minute. It won't take long," Chase replied, clenching her teeth.

She kept a firm grip on the swarm of emotions crowding in on her; thoughts of what it had even taken for her to do this, knowing that she'd come to confront her mother. She now wondered if she would be able to weather the emotional storm that threatened to break if she did.

Even if Maybelle would allow her to.

"Come on in then," Maybelle finally agreed, and Chastity released a sigh of relief.

Maybelle moved aside, opened the door fully and allowed Chase to enter.

"I was in the middle of something, so I ain't got much time to spare," she said again, walking ahead of Chase, her shoulders stooped, giving her an even more frail appearance.

"I know. I won't take much of your time," she replied, following her mother throughout the dark house. There were no lights on until they came to the kitchen. The single light over the oven lit the small room.

Chase entered and stood in the middle of the kitchen, uncertain what to do and where to start.

"Go on and turn on a light, girl," Maybelle said gruffly and glanced away as she walked into the kitchen.

Chase flipped on a light switch and glanced over the kitchen and connecting living room.

Nothing had changed from the last time she'd been there, which had been over ten years ago. The same knick-knacks were set in ornately carved shadow boxes. The same cheap dime-store prints hung on the whitewashed walls. The same old but clean sofa, covered with an afghan, was in the exact same position, still flanked by matching oatmeal-colored chairs. In front of the sofa was a long, cherrywood table where magazines were placed, stacked in the center. Everything was neat and orderly. Everything was pristine. Not an object was out of place.

Chase tugged at the collar of her blouse, pulling it away from her neck. She felt as though she were being choked.

"There's a place for everything, girl, and everything has its place..."

Maybelle's words from years ago came to her mind.

Chase stared at the living room, seeing herself as a young girl, rag in hand as she polished and cleaned the furniture. As she cleaned, she would listen to the kids outside playing and desperately wanted to rebel, to throw the rag away and join them. If she dared to do that, there would be hell to pay.

"What? You too good to sit down at my table? I may not live in that high-siddity uptown place of yours, but my stuff is good enough," Maybelle said gruffly, startling Chase from the long ago images that swam before her eyes.

"Yes, ma'am. I mean, no, ma'am." She stopped. "I'm sorry." The words spilled out of her mouth as though on cue, from some old familiar song. The instant need to apologize was immediate.

She opened her mouth to apologize again for the unknown slight before she clamped her mouth shut. The response had been automatic, one that had reduced her to that little girl she was long ago. The child she'd been, the one who jumped and apologized for any perceived wrong, rather fact or something only in Maybelle's mind.

Chase had to swallow down the bile as her eyes glanced toward the stairs that had once led to her bedroom. Her mother caught her eyes when she turned back around to face her, her dark-brown face flushing before her features hardened and she turned away.

Chase stared at her mother's back as she shuffled over to the oven and removed a tea kettle before filling it with water.

Time hadn't been kind to Maybelle. Barely in her sixties, lines were strongly etched in harsh grooves bracketing her wide, thick lips. Her rheumy eyes were no longer sharp and clear; instead their light-brown depths were worn ragged.

She remembered as a girl how imposing her mother had seemed to her, how indomitable. However, as she watched her mother's slightly stooped form, she now saw her with the eyes of an adult. One no longer afraid of the strident call, harsh tone, or painful blows inflicted on her.

"You want some tea?"

"No. Thank you."

She watched her mother amble around the kitchen, filling the old tea-kettle with water before placing it on the stove to heat.

"So, what do you want? I ain't heard from you in a while. Last time I heard from you, you was working for that place uptown..."

"Manhattan Buford," Chase supplied.

Although she hadn't step foot in the house she grew up in, from the moment she left, there was a small part of her that, despite the years of abuse she'd suffered under her mother's care, hadn't been able to completely divorce her mother from her life.

Like a dutiful daughter, she called her mother every Sunday after she knew Maybelle was home from church to check on her, to find out if there was anything she needed.

The only time Maybelle contacted her was when she needed money. When Chase had offered to bring it to her, Maybelle would cut her short and tell her to wire it although they both lived in the same city.

Chase never questioned why. In truth, she was relieved when she wouldn't have to see her mother. She was able to assuage herself of any guilty feelings by giving her mother money, allowing her money to be the link that kept them connected.

"What you do?" Maybelle turned around, the cup of tea held tightly in her thick fingers.

Chase frowned. "What are you talking about?"

"What you do not to get that promotion you were so sure was yours? What'd you do wrong?" Maybelle asked, her lip curling as she assessed Chase across the room, her watery eyes piercing as she stared at her over the rim of her tea mug. She took a long drink of the tea. Chase stared as the strong column of Maybelle's throat worked the hot liquid down.

"I didn't come here to talk about that." Irritated, unable to keep sitting in the chair, Chase stood and walked toward the living room.

"Sit down somewhere. All that moving around is getting on my nerves. If you didn't come to tell me about that new job, then what you come here for? I already told you, I'm busy," Maybelle mumbled.

Chase didn't bother asking what Maybelle was busy with. She knew it was just her way of trying to get rid of her.

"What did I ever do to you, to make you hate me so, Momma?"

There was a moment of silence after Chase blurted out the words.

"Now look—"

"Why did you let...*him*...do that to me?" She couldn't bring herself to call him father.

Once she started, she couldn't stop.

All the pain, humiliation and fears crowded in on her as her fingers feathered over Maybelle's beloved collectibles all neatly arranged on the shelves. Her fingers slid over the familiar books Maybelle had from the time Chase was a child.

Her eyes zeroed in on the small assortment of photos and bittersweet memories assailed her as she picked up one old photo framed in a chipped ceramic frame.

It was a picture one of the nuns had taken of her at a school outing. Chase remembered she'd been in the first grade and so excited to go on her first field trip. She'd gone to Catholic school and instead of having to wear their traditional plaid skirt and white blouse, the students were allowed to wear street clothes.

Maybelle had carefully dressed Chase, actually buying her a new pair of jeans and T-shirt for the outing. Chase had been so happy, proud of the new clothes, and although she'd wanted to run and play like the other kids, she had been careful not to mess up her new clothes.

She hadn't been looking where she was going and had fallen, tearing the knee of her jeans. When she got home, she'd suffered the consequences.

She placed the picture down and turned to see Maybelle staring at her.

"Why do you hate me so? What did I ever do to make you hate me so bad?"

"What the hell are you going on about, girl? Ain't nobody hate you! I raised you the best I could. I worked night and day to keep a roof over your ungrateful head and all I get is—"

"Why did you let him rape me, over and over, Maybelle? Why?" The words spilled from her in a torrential flood.

"You wasn't listening to me. I thought maybe you'd listen to a man better. You needed discipline. You wasn't listening to me," she mumbled, repeating herself and not looking Chase in the eyes.

"By molesting me? You thought I'd learn *discipline* by allowing my own father to rape me?"

The bitter anger that had been brewing for years overflowed. Tears of anger ran unchecked down her face.

"Shut up! He never did nothing like that, you nasty slut!" Maybelle turned away and fumbled as she began to clumsily attack the dishes, her lined face set in angry lines of denial.

Chase left the living room and strode into the kitchen, staring at Maybelle. She stood several feet away to stare at Maybelle, watching her hands shake as she sank her hands in the soapy water and began to wash the dishes methodically, scrubbing and re-scrubbing the shining plate. Maybelle's eyes were glued to the shining plate.

She threw the dish down in the sink, splattering it in half and moved as though to leave.

Chase reached out a hand and grasped her mother's shoulder, preventing her from leaving.

"Momma, you *knew* what he was doing! Don't stand there and fucking lie to me!"

"Don't you talk to me like that! You shut your lying, filthy mouth!" Maybelle yelled back and with a strength that amazed Chase, shoved at her. In Maybelle's earnest washing, water had overlapped, spilling on the floor, and Chase slipped on it. Before she could right herself, she fell, desperately grasping the handle on a nearby cabinet to stop her fall.

Maybelle stood before her with a sneer on her face.

"See, this is why you needed discipline. You could never control yourself. You was always a deceitful, lying, devious little bitch, and you needed someone to keep you in check."

Chase narrowed her eyes, staring into the malevolent face of her mother.

"Always crying, whining about something. Even as a baby, you were always demanding. I couldn't have a free moment to myself, always sick. There was always *something* with you! You're the reason why he left." Maybelle's ample bosom heaved. Her dark face was flushed in anger as she stared down at Chase.

Chase remained in the half-crouched position, staring into her mother's reddened, angry face.

"If it hadn't been for you, Charlie would have never left. We were fine before you came along, and then when you came, it was never the same. He always found a reason to be gone, said you crying was getting on his nerves. Told me if I didn't get you under control, if I didn't get you to shut up, he was gone."

Her large nostrils flared angrily as she stared down at Chase. Chase knew she was locked in the past and although her eyes were on hers, she didn't see her.

"When he came back, I promised him it would be different."

"It isn't my fault. It was never my fault." Chase slowly rose, a burden being lifted off of her, falling like the useless weight it was as she finally allowed the truth to settle in.

As Maybelle continued to stare down at her, pinning Chase with an evil glare, she felt disdain and pity for the old woman rather than fear. She slowly rose from her crouched position and faced her mother.

She'd dreamed of this day. The day she would have the courage to face her mother and demand answers. The day she'd force the old woman to account for her actions.

Judgment day.

And now, as she faced her, staring down at the woman who'd intimidated her, abused her, allowed her to be abused, instead of vindication, she only felt sadness for the creature in front of her.

A strange euphoria wrapped warmly around her, cocooning her in its embrace as she stood.

Her past of pain and neglect, fear and trepidation were over.

She had faced her demon. The demon that had plagued her, making her always feel as though she was less than the fear that dictated her life, forcing her to make herself rigid in her desire for control over every aspect of her life.

"I feel sorry for you, Maybelle."

"What I got to be sorry for?"

Chase stared at her mother, knowing that Maybelle saw the truth in Chase's eyes. There was no need for an answer. Chase walked over and gathered her things.

She opened her purse and withdrew a small stack of bills, laying them on the counter. Maybelle's greedy eyes shifted to the stack as she licked her lips in obvious anticipation. "This will be the last 'loan' you'll get from me. I'm not giving it to you because I think I 'owe you.' I'm giving it to you because it's my way of saying good-bye to you. I don't hate you. I don't love you. You were a part of my past, a past that I don't need to constantly revisit. A past that I will no longer allow to define me. Good-bye, Maybelle."

Without another word or a final glance, Chase turned and walked away.

Chase thought about saying more, thought about all the things she thought she would say, things she wanted to say in her final say with her mother. But she realized they no longer mattered.

As she walked out of the door to her mother's house for the final time, she knew she'd quieted the demons of her past. Her trip to the island had opened her eyes to the possibilities of living her life without constraints, without the overwhelming need to control everything and everyone in her life.

Maybelle no longer had any power over her.

CHAPTER 19

Chase strode through downtown offices of Manhattan Buford with determined steps. She walked past the open area that was cluttered with at least a dozen small cubicles, not sparing a second look for the curious glances that fell her way.

When she reached the outer door of the mid-managerial team where she had her office, she took a deep breath, briefly closed her eyes, and shouldered her way inside.

Christine glanced up when the door opened, her eyes widening in surprise when she saw Chase.

"Ms. Davidson? I wasn't expecting you…I thought…"

"Yes, I know, Christine," she interrupted quietly. "Is my office still available?" Chase asked, unsure if they'd already assigned someone else to the office.

"Of course! Everything is just like you left it. Can I get you anything? Coffee?" Although Christine was clearly confused, she was the epitome of professionalism as she jumped from her seat and scurried around to the front of her desk.

Chase held up a stalling hand.

"No, I'm fine, Christine." Chase stopped. "You know, coffee sounds good. Your coffee is always perfect." She smiled and turned toward her door, biting back a chuckle when Christine's mouth formed a perfect "O" and her pale face blushed at the small compliment. During the two years that Christine worked for her, Chase had never given the woman the slightest bit of praise. She vowed to rectify that.

If she still had the opportunity, Chase thought and opened the door of her office and gently closed it on her blushing assistant's face.

She leaned back against the door frame, feeling a sense of déjà vu.

Two weeks ago, she'd done the same thing after leaving the meeting with the partners and Javier.

Two weeks ago she'd quit her job when she hadn't gotten the promotion she thought she needed, the one she thought would prove her worth. She'd gathered her things and left, feeling betrayed with her tail tucked beneath her and wondering how things had gotten so out of control, how she'd been left with egg on her face.

Now, she was back and determined to start new. Things that she thought were so important in the past, no longer were. With everything she had learned about herself and the complete turnaround in her feelings about who she was, she felt different, felt empowered. *A true "ah ha" moment as Oprah would say*, Chase thought with an inner laugh.

She took the remainder of the week off, thinking of what she would do next. It hadn't taken long before she realized what she wanted—no, what she *needed*—to do.

She'd made a call to one of the partners, and quietly, with dignity, asked if her job was still open for her, apologizing for her behavior. She hadn't known what to expect, had half expected him to laugh and tell her what she could do with her apology. However, she had been pleasantly surprised when he welcomed her back and asked her if she required any more time off before returning.

She'd assured him she had taken all the time she needed and that she would be returning on Monday.

"And now, here I am," she said aloud, in a barely audible voice, her eyes scanning her office.

Nothing had been moved; everything was exactly as it was when she'd left two weeks earlier. She dropped her jacket on the small, leather chair tucked in the corner and walked toward her desk. Immediately, her eyes widened when she saw the large, bountiful hibiscus plant in a gleaming, burnished gold pot.

With her mouth ajar as she approached the plant, she reached a hand out and ran it over one of the petals that were so large and perfectly formed. They almost appeared as if the fragile petals had been crafted from crepe paper. The petals were so delicate.

A smile stretched her mouth wide, and her heart quickened when she saw the small envelope nestled deep within the plant. She lifted it out of the plant and opened the card. Her brow etched in confusion when she read the card's one line.

Your time to blossom has arrived…

Her door opened. Without looking away from the magnificent plant and her mind puzzling over the note attached, she asked Christine to place her coffee on her desk.

"I don't have any coffee…Hopefully what I do have will bring you a bit more pleasure."

Chase's head whipped around. Stunned, she watched as the man from the island entered her office.

"What are you doing here?" she asked and laughed at the look of affront that crossed his face.

"Should I have made an appointment?" he asked, closing the door and striding into her office.

A thousand questions entered her mind, but none seemed important as he held his arms out to her. Without another word, Chase ran into his arms, and when his head descended and his lips slanted over hers, she willingly sank into the deep, explosively hot kiss.

He pulled her tight into his embrace, his hands roaming over her body as she wrapped her arms around his neck, pulling him tighter and closer as their lips crashed and bodies strained against each other.

It was long minutes before the kiss ended. With reluctance, he withdrew his mouth from hers.

"Of course, you don't need an appointment...But how did you know where I worked? How did you know I'd be here when even I didn't know?" she finally asked, completely out of breath.

"Let's sit down. I have a lot to tell you," he replied, stroking a callused thumb over her kiss-swollen lips.

Confused but happy to see him, Chase allowed him to guide her to the small loveseat in the corner of her office.

"My name is Daemon Baptiste."

It took more than a few seconds for the significance to penetrate her brain.

"Daemon Baptiste?"

He said nothing, staring at her. His gaze remained steady, yet she noted the uncertainty in his eyes as though he was unsure of what reception his announcement would have with her.

"*The* Daemon Baptiste? As in the controlling stockholder of Manhattan Buford?" Her eyes narrowed, staring at him.

"Yes. One and the same."

"What was this, some kind of twisted game?" Chase angrily shoved his hands away and tried to leap from the chaise. He stopped her, grabbing her wrists before she could move and forcing her to turn back to face him.

"No. It wasn't a game, Chase. My intent was never to hurt you. It was the exact opposite," he replied. Although his tone remained the same, his pale gray eyes shone brightly with sincerity.

"Then why..." Her voice trailed off, and she stopped speaking.

She closed her eyes and inhaled a deep breath of air before reopening them and stared at him in anger and confusion. "God, I feel like Alice in damn wonderland! I don't understand any of this!" She angrily pulled her wrists away from him, shoving him away. He allowed her to move from him.

"Please, just hear me out. If after I'm done, you don't want to have anything to do with me or my proposition, you're free to go." He held a hand out in entreaty, silently begging her to stay and to hear him out before she ran as far and as fast as she could away from the madness her life had become.

Wetting her lips, she tucked an errant strand of hair behind her ear, carefully examining his face for any clues to what in hell was going on. She nodded her head, agreeing for him to continue speaking, but she warily watched him.

"I make it my job to know about every member of management, even the junior members. Your work ethic is beyond reproach. Your attention to details, your long hours are all... commendable."

"But?"

He smiled. “No ‘but.’ You reminded me of someone I knew a long time ago. Someone who was just as driven, just as determined to succeed no matter the cost.”

He didn’t say who the person was, but Chase knew he was referring to himself. She allowed him to speak without interruption.

“I admire those strengths. But those same strengths could be the very things that prevent you from fully blossoming.”

She picked up and stroked the hibiscus petal that had fallen onto her desk , tears blurring the image as she stared at it blindly.

“I want more from you, more than you can give. Unless you were freed from the cage you’d placed yourself in, you would never reach your full potential.”

“Were you the one to invite me to the island?”

One side of his wide mouth lightly lifted. “I may have had something do with it. The opportunity arose…”

She didn’t ask for details she knew he wouldn’t give.

“So, I’m to be your assistant?”

He smiled slightly, the lone dimple in one cheek flashing. “You could say that.”

“But the position is a bit more than that of an ‘assistant,’ as the partners led you to believe. I didn’t share with them the full scope of what the position would mean.”

“So. It’s more than making your coffee and taking dictation?”

“You could say that.”

To her utter astonishment, he outlined the scope of her duties. Her main one was to run the Dallas office of Manhattan Buford, a position that would give her full autonomy in every final decision the firm had.

“Of course that comes with your own staff, a fantastic raise, of course, an office with an incredible view…”

Chase listened as he detailed entirely the scope of her new job and all the responsibilities that went with it. Her mind was whirling, emotions—astonishment and euphoria—were crashing in on her as she was blown away with the magnitude of his gesture. Of his obvious faith in her as a leader and her abilities to lead the company.

Two weeks ago, her world had closed in on her. Now, she was being handed the golden key. A key that would give her the opportunity to show that she indeed had what it took to run an entire branch of a multibillion-dollar corporation.

She stared at the man who was the catalyst to turmoil in her life. Turmoil was needed to force her to come to terms with her life, to re-evaluate who she was. In doing so, he not only helped to free herself of the demons of her past, but had also helped her realize the possibilities of a future she never dreamed of.

She had plenty of questions—about the position, as well as questions about the man who sat staring at her. But all of those could wait for the moment.

"Does this sound like something you'd be interested in, Ms. Davidson?" he asked, a small smile flirting around his sensual mouth.

Chase laughed out loud, beyond satisfied with the unexpected outcome. "Yes…It is."

ABOUT THE AUTHOR

Kimberly Kaye Terry is a multi-published author who pens interracial and multicultural delicious tales that expertly blend eroticism and true romance, as well as erotic fiction. She lives with her husband, a Lieutenant Colonel in the U.S. Army, their beautiful child, and two ridiculously spoiled poodles who think they're human, in a suburb in Texas.

Although Kimberly has a bachelor's degree in social work and a master's degree in human relations, and has held licenses in social work and mental health therapy in various cities within the United States and abroad, she happily calls writing her full-time job. Kimberly volunteers at various social service agencies and is a longstanding member of Zeta Phi Beta Sorority, Inc., a community-conscious organization.

Kimberly is a naturalist and practices aromatherapy. She believes in embracing the powerful woman within each of us and meditates on a regular basis. You can visit her at www.kimberlykayeterry.com to learn more about her. Or feel free to drop by her MySpace blog, where she occasionally waxes poetic, or shamelessly pimps her books, at www.myspace.com/kimberlykayeterry.